A BOY CALLED CHRISTMAS

MATT HAIG

with illustrations by CHRIS MOULD

CANONGATE

For Lucas and Pearl

This paperback edition published in 2021 by Canongate Books

First published in Great Britain in 2015 by
Canongate Books Ltd, 14 High Street, Edinburgh EH1 1TE

canongate.co.uk

1

British Library Cataloguing-in-Publication Data
A catalogue record for this book is available on
request from the British Library

ISBN 978 1 83885 372 3
Export ISBN 978 1 83885 701 1

Typeset in 13.25/15pt Bembo by
Palimpsest Book Production Ltd, Falkirk, Stirlingshire

Printed and bound in Great Britain by Clays Ltd, Elcograf S.p.A.

A BOY CALLED CHRISTMAS

Matt Haig has won the Blue Peter Book Award, the Smarties Book Prize and been nominated three times for the Carnegie Medal for his stories for children. He is also a number one bestselling writer for adults. The first book in his festive series, *A Boy Called Christmas*, has been made into a feature film with an all-star cast.

Chris Mould went to art school at the age of sixteen and has been drawing ever since. He has won the Nottingham Children's Book Award, the Swiss Prix Enfantaisie award and twice been shortlisted for the Kate Greenaway Medal.

Also by Matt Haig

Shadow Forest
The Runaway Troll
To Be a Cat
Echo Boy
The Girl Who Saved Christmas
Father Christmas and Me
The Truth Pixie
Evie and the Animals
The Truth Pixie Goes to School
Evie in the Jungle
A Mouse Called Miika

A Note from the Author

Dear Reader,

When my son, Lucas, was six years old he asked me a question.

He always asked me questions. He still does, at thirteen, but not quite as many as he did back then. The light had just gone out in his bedroom, and his voice floated through the dark.

'Dad, what was Father Christmas like as a boy?'

It was a good question. But it was late and I was tired and it was past his bedtime.

'I don't know,' I told him. 'I have never really thought about it.'

But there is a certain type of question that doesn't go away. And this was one of them. And so I went away and *wrote* an answer. An answer that threaded together all the important things – the magic powers, the red hat, the reindeer, the elves, the *hope* – and added a few new things too, like the Truth Pixie and a certain mouse.

But when you write a book you have no idea what it will become. And I had no idea that the story would be beautifully illustrated by Chris

Mould. Or that it would have lots of readers. Or be turned into a movie.

A movie.

It was a dream to watch the filming. To go and walk around elf houses and an elf school. To see hundreds of people making a big bright film that began as a small question asked in the dark.

I love the film. I love that the director Gil Kenan was inspired by the story, adding some fantastic new bits, but always staying true to the heart of the tale. It was so amazing to see the story take on a new life, with some of the most brilliant actors on the planet.

I hope you enjoy the film and the book. And if you do, you might also like the next books in the series – *The Girl Who Saved Christmas* and *Father Christmas and Me*, which were just as exciting to write. Or, if you are a mouse kind of person, you might like to read the newest story – *A Mouse Called Miika*.

It has been the best fun of my writing life, to be able to head into Elfhelm and find some magic there whenever it is needed.

I hope you find a little magic there too.

Merry Christmas!

Matt Haig

A
BOY
CALLED
CHRISTMAS

Impossible.
  – An old elf swear word

An Ordinary Boy

You are about to read the true story of Father Christmas.

Yes. Father Christmas.

You may wonder how I know the true story of Father Christmas, and I will tell you that you shouldn't really question such things. Not right at the start of a book. It's rude, for one thing. All you need to understand is that I do know the story of Father Christmas, or else why would I be writing it?

Maybe you don't call him Father Christmas.

Maybe you call him something else.

Santa or Saint Nick or Santa Claus or Sinterklaas or Kris Kringle or Pelznickel or Papa Noël or Strange Man With A Big Belly Who Talks To Reindeer And Gives Me Presents. Or maybe you have a name you've come up with yourself, just for fun. If you were an elf, though, you would always call him Father Christmas. It was the pixies who started calling him Santa Claus, and spread the word, just to confuse things, in their mischievous way.

But whatever you happen to call him, you know about him, and that's the main thing.

Can you believe there was a time when no one knew about him? A time when he was just an ordinary boy called Nikolas, living in the middle of nowhere, or the middle of Finland, doing nothing with magic except believing in it? A boy who knew very little about the world except the taste of mushroom soup, the feel of a cold north wind, and the stories he was told. And who only had a doll made out of a turnip to play with.

But life was going to change for Nikolas, in ways he could never have imagined. Things were going to happen to him.

Good things.

Bad things.

Impossible things.

But if you are one of those people who believe that some things are impossible, you should put this book down right away. It is most certainly not for you.

Because this book is full of *impossible things*.

Are you still reading the book?
Good. (Elves would be proud.)
Then let us begin . . .

A Woodcutter's Son

Now, Nikolas was a happy boy. Well, actually, no.

He would have told you he was happy, if you asked him, and he certainly *tried* to be happy, but sometimes being happy is quite tricky. I suppose, what I am saying is that Nikolas was a boy who believed in happiness, the way he believed in elves and trolls and pixies, but he had never actually seen an elf or a troll or a pixie, and he hadn't really seen proper happiness either. At least, not for a very long time. He didn't have it that easy. Take Christmas.

This is the list of every present Nikolas had received for Christmas. In his entire life.

1. A wooden sleigh.
2. A doll carved out of a turnip.

That's it.

The truth is that Nikolas's life was hard. But he made the best of it.

He had no brothers or sisters to play with, and the nearest town − Kristiinankaupunki (Kris-tee-nan-cow-punky) − was a long way away. It took even longer to get to than it did to pronounce. And anyway there wasn't much to do in Kristiinankaupunki except go to church or look in the window of the toyshop.

'Papa! Look! A wooden reindeer!' Nikolas would gasp as he pressed his nose against the glass of that toyshop.

Or,

'Look! An elf doll!'

Or,

'Look! A cuddly doll of the king!'

And once he even asked,

'Can I have one?'

He looked up at his father's face. A long and thin face with thick bushy eyebrows and skin rougher than old shoes in the rain.

'Do you know how much it is?' said Joel, his father.

'No,' said Nikolas.

And then his father held up his left hand, fingers stretched. He only had four and a half fingers on his left hand because of an accident with an axe. A horrible accident. Lots of

9

blood. And we probably shouldn't dwell on it too much, as this is a Christmas story.

'Four and a half rubles?'

His father looked cross. 'No. *No*. Five. Five rubles. And five rubles for an elf doll is too much money. You could buy a cottage for that.'

'I thought cottages cost one hundred rubles, Papa?'

'Don't try and be clever, Nikolas.'

'I thought you said I should try and be clever.'

'Not right now,' said his father. 'And anyway, why would you need an elf doll when you have that turnip-doll your mother made? Couldn't you pretend the turnip is an elf?'

'Yes, Papa, of course,' Nikolas said, because he didn't want to make his father upset.

'Don't worry, son. I'll work so hard that one day I'll be rich and you can have all the toys you want and we can have a *real* horse, with our own coach, and ride into town like a king and a prince!'

'Don't work too hard, Papa,' said Nikolas. 'You need to play sometimes too. And I *am* happy with my turnip-doll.'

But his father had to work hard. Chopping

wood all day and every day. He worked as soon as it was light to when it was dark.

'The trouble is we live in Finland,' his father explained, on the day our story starts.

'Doesn't everyone live in Finland?' asked Nikolas.

It was morning. They were heading out into the forest, passing the old stone well that they could never look at. The ground was dusted with a thin layer of snow. Joel had an axe on his back. The blade dazzled in the cold morning sun.

'No,' said Joel. 'Some people live in Sweden. And there are about seven people who live in Norway. Maybe even eight. The world is a big place.'

'So what is the problem with living in Finland, Papa?'

'Trees.'

'Trees? I thought you liked trees. That's why you chop them down.'

'But there are trees everywhere. So no one pays much for . . .' Joel stopped. Turned around.

'What is it, Papa?'

'I thought I heard something.' They saw nothing but birch and pine trees and shrubs of herbs and heather. A tiny red-breasted bird sat on a branch.

'Must have been nothing,' Joel said, unsure.

Joel stared up at a giant pine, pressed his hand on the rough bark. 'This is the one.' He began chopping, and Nikolas began his search for mushrooms and berries.

Nikolas only had a single mushroom in his basket when he caught a glimpse of an animal in the distance. Nikolas loved animals, but mainly saw only birds, mice and rabbits. Sometimes he would see a moose.

But this was something bigger and stronger.

A bear. A giant brown bear, about three times the size of Nikolas, standing on its hind legs, its huge paws scooping berries into its mouth. Nikolas's heart started a drum roll with excitement. He decided to get a closer look.

He walked quietly forward. He was quite close now.

I know that bear!

The terrifying moment when he realised he recognised the bear was also the one where he stepped on a twig and it cracked. The bear turned, stared straight at him.

Nikolas felt something grab his arm, hard. He turned to see his father looking crossly down at him.

'What are you doing?' he hissed. 'You'll get yourself killed.'

His dad's grip was so tight it hurt. But then he let go.

'Be the forest,' whispered Joel. This was something he always said, whenever danger was around. Nikolas never knew what it meant. He just stayed still. But it was too late.

Nikolas remembered when he was six years old with his mother – his jolly, singing, rosy-cheeked mother. They had been going to get

some water from the well when they'd seen the exact same bear. His mother had told Nikolas to run back to the cottage, and Nikolas had run. She hadn't.

Nikolas watched his father hold his axe with a stronger grip, but he saw his father's hands tremble. He pulled Nikolas back, behind him, in case the bear charged.

'Run,' his father said.

'No. I'm staying with you.'

It was unclear if the bear was going to chase them. It probably wasn't. It was probably too old and tired. But it did roar at them.

Then, right at that moment, there was a whistling sound. Nikolas felt something brush against his ear, like a fast feather. A moment later, a grey-feathered arrow pierced the tree beside the bear's head. The bear went down on all fours, and sloped away.

Nikolas and Joel looked behind them, trying to see who had fired the arrow, but there was nothing but pine trees.

'It must be the hunter,' said Joel.

A week before, they had found an injured moose with the same grey-feathered arrow sticking out of it. Nikolas had made his father help the poor creature. He'd watched him gather snow and press it around the wound before pulling the arrow out.

They kept staring through the trees. A twig cracked, but they didn't see anything.

'All right, Christmas, let's go,' Joel said.

Nikolas hadn't been called that for a long time.

Back in the old days his father used to joke about and have fun. He used to call everyone nicknames. Nikolas's mother was 'Sweetbread' even though her real name was Lilja, and Nikolas himself was nicknamed 'Christmas' because he had been born on Christmas Day. His father had even engraved his wooden sleigh with the nickname.

'Look at him, Sweetbread, our little boy Christmas.'

He was hardly ever called that now.

'But don't ever go spying on bears, okay? You'll get yourself killed. Stay near me. You're still clearly a boy.'

A little later, after Joel had been chopping for an hour, he sat down on a tree stump.

'I could help you,' offered Nikolas.

His father held up his left hand. 'This is what happens when eleven-year-olds use axes.'

So Nikolas just kept his eyes to the ground,

looking for mushrooms, and wondered if being eleven years old was ever going to be any fun.

The Cottage and the Mouse

The cottage where Nikolas and Joel lived was the second smallest cottage in the whole of Finland.

It only had one room. So the bedroom was also the kitchen and the living room and the bathroom. Actually, there was no bath. There wasn't even a toilet. The toilet was just a massive deep hole in the ground outside. The house had two beds, with mattresses stuffed with straw and feathers. The sledge was always kept outside, but Nikolas kept his turnip-doll beside the bed to remind him of his mother.

But Nikolas didn't mind. It didn't really matter how small a house was if you had a big imagination. And Nikolas spent his time daydreaming and thinking of magical things like pixies and elves.

The best part of Nikolas's day was bedtime, because this was when his father would tell him a story. A little brown mouse, who Nikolas

named Miika, would sneak into the warmth of the cottage and listen too.

Well, Nikolas liked to think that Miika was listening but really he was just fantasising about cheese. Which took quite a lot of fantasising, as Miika was a forest mouse, and there weren't any cows or goats in this forest, and he had never seen or smelt cheese, let alone tasted it.

But Miika, like all mice, believed in the existence of cheese, and knew it would taste very, very good if he got such an opportunity.

Anyway, Nikolas would lie there, in the happy cosiness of his bedclothes, and listen intently to his father's stories. Joel always looked tired. He had rings under his eyes. He seemed to get a new one every year. Like a tree.

'Now,' said his father, that night. 'What story would you like tonight?'

'I'd like you to tell me about the elves.'

'Again? You've been told about the elves every night since you were three.'

'Please, Papa. I like to hear about them.'

So Joel told a story about the elves of the Far North, who lived beyond the only mountain in Finland, a secret mountain, that some people doubt is there. The elves lived in a magical land, a snow-covered village called Elfhelm surrounded by wooded hills.

'Are they real, Papa?' Nikolas asked.

'Yes. I've never seen them,' his father said, sincerely, 'but I believe they are. And sometimes believing is as good as knowing.'

And Nikolas agreed, but Miika the mouse disagreed, or he would have done if he had understood. If he had understood he would have said 'I'd rather taste real cheese than just believe in it.'

But for Nikolas, it was enough. 'Yes, Papa, I know believing is as good as knowing. I believe the elves are friendly. Do you?'

'Yes,' said Joel. 'And they wear brightly coloured clothes.'

'You wear colourful clothes, Papa!'

This was true, but Joel's clothes were made from leftover rags he got for free from the tailor's in town. He had made himself multi-coloured patchwork trousers and a green shirt and – best of all – a big floppy red hat with a white furry rim and a fluffy white cotton bobble.

'Oh yes, I do, but my clothes are getting old and tatty. The elves' clothes always look brand new and . . .'

He stopped right there.

There was a noise outside.

And a moment later came three hard knocks on the door.

The Hunter

That's strange,' said Joel.

'Maybe it's Aunt Carlotta,' said Nikolas, really hoping more than anything in the world that it wasn't Aunt Carlotta.

Joel walked over to the door. It wasn't a long walk. It only took him one step. He opened the door to reveal a man.

A tall, strong, broad-shouldered, square-jawed man with hair like golden straw. He had bright blue eyes and smelt of hay and looked as powerful as twenty horses. Or half a bear. He looked strong enough to lift the cottage off the ground, if that had been what he wanted. But he wasn't in the mood for lifting cottages off the ground today.

They recognised the arrows the man was carrying on his back, and their grey feathers.

'It's you,' said Joel. 'The hunter.'

Nikolas could see his father was impressed.

'It is,' said the man. Even his voice sounded

like it had muscles. 'My name is Anders. That was a pretty close thing with the bear earlier.'

'Yes, thank you. Come in, come in. I'm Joel. And this is my good son Nikolas.'

The big man noticed the mouse sitting in the corner of the room, eating a mushroom.

'I don't like you,' said Miika, looking at the man's large shoes. 'Your feet are, frankly, terrifying.'

'Would you like a drink?' Joel asked, meekly. 'I have some cloudberry wine.'

'Yes,' said Anders, and then he saw Nikolas and smiled in a friendly way at him. 'Wine would be nice. I see that you wear your red hat even indoors, Joel.'

'Well, it keeps me warm.'

Cloudberry wine, thought Nikolas, as Joel pulled down a bottle that was hiding on the top of the kitchen cupboard. He didn't know his father had any cloudberry wine.

Fathers were mysteries.

'I've come to ask if you can help with something,' said Anders.

'Ask away,' Joel said, pouring out two cups of wine.

Anders took a sip. Then a gulp. Then he drank the entire cup. He wiped his mouth with his big right hand. 'I want you to do something. Something for the king.'

Joel was startled. 'King Frederick?' Then he laughed. This was clearly dark hunter humour. 'Ha! For a minute there I actually believed you! What on this Earth would a king require from a humble woodcutter like myself?'

Joel waited for Anders to laugh too, but there was a long silence.

'I've been watching you all day. You're good with an axe . . .' Anders trailed off, seeing that Nikolas was sitting up in bed with wide open eyes listening to the most exciting conversation he'd ever heard. 'Maybe we should talk in private.'

Joel nodded so hard the white bobble on his hat fell forward. 'Nikolas, could you go in the other room?'

'But, Papa, we don't *have* another room.'

His father sighed. 'Oh yes. You're right . . . Well,' he said to his giant guest, 'maybe we should go outside. It's quite a mild summer night. You can borrow my hat if you want.'

Anders laughed loud and long. 'I think I'll survive without it!'

And so the men went outside and Nikolas went to bed, straining to hear what they said. He listened to the voices murmuring and he could just pick out the odd word.

'. . . men . . . king . . . rubles . . . Turku . . . long . . . mountain . . . weapons . . . distance . . . money . . . money . . .' Money was mentioned

29

a few times. But then he heard a word that made him sit up in bed. A magical word. Maybe the most magical word of all. '*Elves.*'

Nikolas saw Miika scuttling along the edge of the floor. He stood up on his back legs, stared at Nikolas, and looked ready to have a conversation. Well, he looked as ready as a mouse ever looks to have a conversation. Which wasn't much.

'Cheese,' said the mouse, in mouse language.

'I've got a very bad feeling about all this, Miika.'

Miika looked up at the window, and Nikolas thought his tiny dark eyes seemed filled with worry, and that his nose was twitching nervously.

'And if I can't have cheese I'll eat this stinky old vegetable creature instead.'

Miika turned to the turnip-doll lying by Nikolas's bed, and took a bite.

'Hey, that was a Christmas present!' said Nikolas.

'I'm a mouse. Christmas means nothing to me.'

'Hey!' said Nikolas again, but it was hard to be cross with a mouse, so he let Miika carry on, nibbling the turnip-doll's ear off.

The men stayed outside the window for

a long time, talking distant words and drinking cloudberry wine, as Nikolas lay there, worried, in the dark, with a bad feeling in his stomach.

Miika also had a bad feeling in his stomach. But that was what you get from eating raw turnip.

'Good night, Miika.'

'I wish it had been cheese,' said Miika.

And Nikolas lay there, with a horrible thought. The thought was this: *Something Bad Is Going To Happen.*

And he was right.

It was.

The Sleigh (and Other Bad News)

Listen, son, I have something I must tell you,' said his father, as they ate stale rye bread for breakfast. This was Nikolas's second favourite breakfast (right after *un-stale* rye bread).

'What is it, Papa? What did Anders want to ask you?'

Joel took a deep breath, as if the next sentence was something he had to swim through. 'I've been offered a job,' he said. 'It's a lot of money. It could be the answer to everything. But . . .'

Nikolas waited, holding his breath. And then it came.

'But I'll have to go away.'

'What?'

'Don't worry. It won't be a long time. Only two months.'

'Two *months*?'

Joel had a bit of a think. 'Three, at the most.'

That sounded like for ever. 'What kind of job takes three months?'

'It's an expedition. A group of men are heading to the Far North. They want to find Elfhelm.'

Nikolas could hardly believe what he was hearing. His mind was spinning with excitement. He had always believed in elves, but never really imagined that people could actually go and see them. *Elves*. Living, breathing *elves*. 'The elf village?'

His father nodded. 'The king has said there's a reward for anyone who finds proof of the elf village. Twelve thousand rubles. Between seven men that's over three thousand each.'

'I don't think it is,' said Nikolas.

'We'd never ever have to worry about money again!'

'Wow! Can I come? I can spot a mushroom from a mile away even in the snow! I'll be really, really useful.'

His father's long leathery face looked sad. The skin under his eyes had gained another ring. His eyebrows were sliding apart like caterpillars falling out of love. Even his dirty old red hat seemed floppier and sadder than usual.

'It's too dangerous,' Joel said, his breath smelling of sour cloudberries. 'And I'm not just talking about bears . . . There will be many nights sleeping out in the cold. Finland is a large country. A hundred miles north of here, there is a village called Seipäjärvi. Beyond that, nothing but iced plains and lakes and snow-covered fields. Even the forests are frozen. And by the time you reach Lapland food – even mushrooms – will be hard to find. And then the journey gets even more difficult. Which is why no one has ever made it to the Far North.'

Tears filled Nikolas's eyes, but he was determined not to cry. He stared at his father's hand, and the missing half finger. 'So how do *you* know you'll make it?'

'There are six other men. Good strong men, I am told. We have as good a chance as anyone.' He gave his familiar crinkly-eyed smile. 'It will be worth it. I promise you. We'll make a lot of money on this expedition, which means we will never have to have watery mushroom soup and stale bread again.'

Nikolas knew his father was sad, and didn't want to make him feel any worse. He knew he must be brave.

'I'll miss you, Papa . . . But I understand that you must go.'

'You're a child of the forest,' Joel said, his voice trembling. 'You've a tough spirit. But remember, you mustn't go near danger. You must stop your curiosity. You have too much courage . . . I'll be back by September, when the weather gets worse. And we'll eat like the king himself!' He held up a piece of dry rye bread in disgust. 'Sausages and fresh buttered bread and mountains of bilberry pie!'

'And cheese?' wondered Miika, but no one heard.

Bilberry pie! Nikolas nearly fainted at the thought. He was so hungry that the idea of the sweet purple berries encrusted in mouthwatering pastry seemed like heaven itself. He'd once tasted a bilberry, and it had been lovely, but everyone knew that the way to make something even lovelier was to put it in a pie. But then he became sad again, and a thought occurred to him. Surely Joel – who was scared to let Nikolas out of his sight sometimes – wouldn't be leaving him on his own.

'Who'll look after me?'

'Don't worry!' said Joel. 'I'll write to my sister. She'll keep you safe.'

Sister! Oh no. This was even worse. It was bad enough spending the whole of Christmas afternoon with Aunt Carlotta, let alone spending three whole months with her.

'It's all right. I can be on my own. I'm a child of the forest. I can . . .'

Now his father interrupted him. 'No. It's a dangerous world. And you're still a child. We saw that yesterday. Aunt Carlotta is a lonely woman. She's a lot older than me. She's really an old lady now. She's forty-two. Hardly anyone lives to be forty-two. It'll be nice for her to have somebody to look after.'

He looked at his son for a long while before breaking the final piece of bad news. 'Oh, and I'll need to take your sleigh. Anders thought it would be useful. To hold our . . . supplies. And anyway, it is summer! The snow is too thin on the ground around here.'

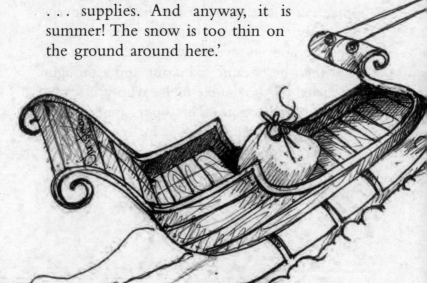

Nikolas nodded. He could not think of an answer.

'You still have your turnip-doll.' Joel pointed to the sad-looking turnip with a face carved in it that was sitting by Nikolas's bed.

'Yes,' said Nikolas. He supposed that as turnip-dolls go it was a very nice one.

Maybe it was the best doll made out of a rotten, stinking turnip in the whole of Finland. 'That's true. I still have that.'

And so, ten days later, on a cold but sunny morning, Nikolas watched his father leave.

Joel was wearing his red hat, carrying his axe on his back and dragging the wooden sleigh behind him. He headed off under a pink sky, through the tall pine trees, to meet the other men in Kristiinankaupunki.

And then, after that, the *really* bad things started to happen.

The Arrival of Aunt Carlotta

Even at a time when most aunts were nasty and horrible, Aunt Carlotta was *particularly* bad.

She was a tall grey-clothed thin woman, with white hair and a long stern face and a very tiny mouth like a full stop. Everything about her, even her voice, seemed covered in frost.

'Now,' she said, sternly, 'it is important we set some rules. The first rule is that you must wake up with the sunrise.'

Nikolas gasped. This was horrible. Finland was in summer! 'But the sun rises in the middle of the night!'

'The second rule is that you do not answer me back. Ever. Especially about the first rule.'

Aunt Carlotta looked at Miika, who had just climbed up the table leg and was now scuttling across the table looking for crumbs. She seemed disgusted.

'And the third rule,' she said, 'is no rats!'

'He's not a rat!'

But it was too late. She had picked Miika the mouse up by his tail and carried the struggling creature to the door, which she opened, before throwing him outside.

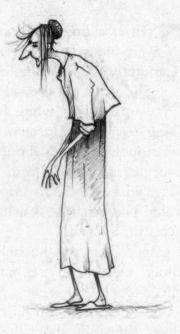

'Hey! You can't do that!' shouted Miika, at the top of his voice. But as the top of Miika's voice was nowhere near the *bottom* of most people's voices no one heard him. She closed the door, sniffed the air and her eyes landed on the turnip-doll by Nikolas's bed.

She picked it up. 'And no horrible rotten vegetables either!'

'It's a doll. Look. It's got a face on it!'

'Actually, on second thoughts, I'll keep it. Might distract me from the smell of you.'

Aunt Carlotta considered Nikolas with even more contempt than she had shown the rotten turnip. 'I'd forgotten how much I *hate* children. Especially boys. I find them . . . *revolting*. It's becoming as clear as the air. My ignorant nine-fingered brother has been too soft with you.'

She looked around the small one-roomed cottage. 'Do you know why I came?' she asked.

'Did he tell you?'

'To look after me.'

'Ha! Ha! Hahahahaha!' Her laugh flapped out of her, suddenly and scarily, like bats from a cave. It was the first and last time he would ever hear her laugh. 'To look after you! Oh, that's good. That's *funny*. What a world you must live in, to think people just do good things for no reason! Do you really think I came here because I *cared* about you? No.

I did not come here for a skinny, grubby childish fool. I came here for the money.'

'The money?'

'Yes. Your father has promised me five hundred rubles on his return. That could buy me five cottages.'

'What would you need five cottages for?'

'To make more money. And then more money . . .'

'Is money all that matters?'

'Spoken like a true grubby little pauper! Now, where do you sleep?'

'There,' said Nikolas, pointing first at his bed

and then to the other end of the room. 'And that's where Papa sleeps.'

Aunt Carlotta shook her head. 'No.'

'I don't understand,' said Nikolas.

'I can't have you in here, seeing me in my undergarments! And besides, I have a very bad back. I need both mattresses. You don't want it to get worse, do you?'

'No, of course not,' said Nikolas.

'Good. So yes, you will sleep outside.'

'*Outside?*'

'Yes. Outside. Fresh air is good for the soul. I never understand why children want to be indoors all the time these days. I know it's nearly the nineteenth century, but still. Go on. Shoosh! It's getting dark.'

So that night, Nikolas lay on the grass outside his house. He had taken his mother's old winter coat to sleep under, and lay on the smoothest patch of grass he could find, between two tree stumps his father had chopped years ago, but there were always pebbles somewhere under his back. The wind blew. He watched Aunt Carlotta in the distance squat over the hole in the ground, hoisting up her petticoat to go to the toilet, and he hoped she'd fall in, then hated himself for thinking that. She went back into the warm cottage, and he shivered under a sky full of twinkling stars, as he clutched his rotten turnip for comfort. He started to think about the unfairness of the universe, and wished there was some way of making it fair again. And as he thought, Miika crept over and joined him, crawling over his arm and resting on his chest.

'I feel sorry for Aunt Carlotta,' he said. 'It can't feel nice to be that miserable. Can it?'

'I don't know,' said Miika.

Nikolas gazed up at the night. Even though he had nothing much to be happy about, he liked to have such sights to look at. A shooting star fell through the sky.

'Did you see that, Miika? It means we have to make a wish.'

So Nikolas wished for a way of replacing meanness with goodness.

'Do you believe in magic, Miika?'

'I believe in cheese, if that counts,' said Miika.

There was no way of Nikolas knowing for sure if the mouse did or didn't believe in magic but, comforted by hope, Nikolas and his little rodent friend managed to fall slowly and gently asleep, as the cold breeze kept blowing, and whispering all the unknown secrets of the night.

Rumbling Stomachs and
Other Nightmares

Nikolas slept outside all summer.

He spent every day – as Aunt Carlotta told him to do – looking for food, from first light until nightfall. One day he saw the bear again. The bear stood upright. But Nikolas waited. Stayed calm. *Be the forest.* The bear stood there, peaceful and terrifying all at once. The bear that had chased his mother towards the well. But he couldn't hate this creature.

'Look at me,' said Nikolas. 'I'm skinny as a rake. No meat on my bones.' The bear seemed to agree, and ambled away on all fours. Was there an unluckier boy in the world? Yes, actually, there was. There was a boy called Gatu who lived in India who'd been struck by lightning while going to the toilet in a stream. Very nasty. But even so, it *was* a miserable joyless time for Nikolas. Aunt Carlotta was never happy with the mushrooms and herbs he managed to find. The only real comfort – apart from Miika – was in counting down the days and weeks and months until his father returned, which he did by scratching lines in the nearest pine tree to the cottage.

Two months passed. Then three. 'Where are you?' he'd ask, amid the trees. The only sound that came back to him was that of the wind, or a distant woodpecker.

Aunt Carlotta became nastier with the days, like vinegar getting more sour. She'd scream at him for nothing.

'Stop that!' shouted Aunt Carlotta one evening, as she ate the soup he had made for her. 'Or I'll feed you to a bear.'

'Stop what?'

'Those horrible noises from inside your disgusting body.'

Nikolas was confused. The only way to stop

a rumbling stomach was by eating, and as with most days he'd only found enough mushrooms for Aunt Carlotta to have soup. And the ones he'd sneaked in his mouth in the forest hadn't been enough.

But then, Aunt Carlotta smiled. A smile on her face was an unusual thing to see, like a banana in the snow. 'All right, you can have some soup.'

'Oh thank you, Aunt Carlotta! I'm so hungry and I love mushroom soup.'

Aunt Carlotta shook her head. 'As you always make me soup I thought I would repay the favour. So, while you were out in the forest, I made some soup especially for you.'

Miika was looking through the window. 'Don't eat it!' he squeaked, pointlessly.

Nikolas looked worried as he stared down at the murky grey-brown liquid. 'What is it made with?' he asked.

'Love,' said Aunt Carlotta.

Nikolas knew she had to be joking. Aunt Carlotta couldn't love any more than an icicle could love. That's a bit unfair to icicles. Icicles melt. Aunt Carlotta was as frozen as a frozen thing that was very frozen and would never melt.

'Go on then. Eat it.'

It was the most disgusting thing he had ever tasted. It was like eating mud and dirt and puddle water. But he could feel Aunt Carlotta watching him, so he kept eating.

Aunt Carlotta's cold grey eyes made Nikolas feel a hundred times smaller than he was as she said for what seemed like the hundredth time, 'Your father is foolish.'

Nikolas didn't answer her back. He just kept sipping the foul soup, feeling more and more sick.

But Aunt Carlotta wasn't going to leave it there. 'Everybody knows there are no such things as elves,' she said, spitting as she spoke. 'Your father is a stupid ignorant child to believe such things. I'd be very surprised if he is still alive. No one has ever been to the Far North and returned to tell the tale. I was so stupid, coming here, waiting for five hundred rubles that will never arrive.'

'You can always go home.'

'Oh no. I can't now. It's October. The weather has turned. I can't walk ten miles in this weather. I'm here all winter now. For Christmas. Not that Christmas means anything to me. It's a hateful time of year.'

This was just too much.

'Christmas is great,' Nikolas said. 'I love Christmas, and don't even care that it clashes with my birthday.' He was going to say 'The only thing that spoils Christmas is you' but he thought better of it.

Aunt Carlotta seemed genuinely confused. 'How can you, a grubby dirty motherless boy, love Christmas? If you were a rich merchant's son in Turku or Helsinki then I could understand it, but my brother has always been too poor to buy you a present!'

Nikolas felt a red flush of anger tingle his skin. 'It was always magical. And I would rather a toy that was made with love, than one that cost a lot of money.'

'But the only thing he ever made you was the sleigh. He was always too busy working.'

Nikolas thought of his old turnip-doll and wondered where it was. It wasn't beside the door where he had left it.

'Your father is a liar.'

'No,' said Nikolas. He had finished the soup but now felt extremely ill.

'He promised you he'd come back. He told you that elves were real. Two lies, right there . . . Anyway, I'm tired now,' said his aunt. 'It's time for my bed. So, now that you've finished

51

your soup, if you can kindly get out of my sight that would make me as happy as the Queen of Finland. This is my house now. I am your guardian. So I'd start doing exactly what I say, exactly as I say it. Get out. Go.'

Nikolas stood up, his stomach aching. He looked around the room. 'Where *is* my turnip-doll?'

Aunt Carlotta smiled. It was a proper smile, and one that was soon turning into a laugh. And then she said it.

'You've just eaten him.'

'What?'

It took a second. No. Two seconds. Maybe three. Three and a half. Actually, no. Just three. But then Nikolas realised what she had just said. His only toy in the world was now in his stomach.

He ran outside and threw up in the toilet hole.

'Why did you do that?' he asked, in disbelief, from outside. 'My mum made me that!'

'Well, she's no longer here, is she?' said Aunt Carlotta, through the small window which she had opened to get a better view of Nikolas being sick. 'Thank the Lord. Used to give me a headache, listening to her bad singing all day. I just thought it was about time you should grow up and leave silly toys behind.'

Nikolas had finished. He went back inside. He thought of his mother. He thought of her holding onto the chain that held the bucket as she tried to escape the bear. How dare Aunt Carlotta say nasty things about her? There was only one option now. To run away. He could not stay here with Aunt Carlotta. He *would* prove his father wasn't a liar, and there was only one way to do it.

'Goodbye, Aunt Carlotta,' he said, just a whisper, under his breath, but he meant it. He was going. He was going to find his father. He was going to see the elves. He was going to make everything all right.

A Very Short Chapter with a Long Title in which Not Very Much Happens

Aunt Carlotta mumbled something and didn't look back at him as she climbed into her bed with two mattresses.

Nikolas took some of the stale bread lying on the table, stuffed it in his pocket, and went outside, into the cold night. He was tired. His stomach still ached and his tongue tasted of rotten turnip but he was also something else – *determined*. Yes. He was going to start the walk to the Far North.

Miika was nibbling on a dry leaf.

The mouse, he supposed, was the closest thing he had to a friend.

'I'm going to the Far North. It'll be a very long and dangerous journey. There's a very high chance of death. I think you should stay here, Miika. It'll be warmer, but if you want to come with me, give me a signal.'

Miika looked, anxiously, at the door to the cottage.

'You don't have to stay right *here*,' Nikolas told him. 'You have the whole forest.'

Miika glanced at the whole forest. 'But there's no cheese in the forest.'

Nikolas still could not speak mouse, but got the general gist. 'So you want to come with me?'

Miika perched on his hind legs and, though Nikolas couldn't be entirely sure, it seemed that the mouse nodded his little head. And so he picked him up and put him in his left-hand coat pocket.

Then, with Miika peeking out at the road ahead, Nikolas turned and headed north through the trees, towards the place he thought he might find his father and the elves, and tried his hardest to believe in both.

The Old Lady

He walked all night and all of the next day. He looked out for the tall brown bear, and saw paw prints in the ground, but not the creature itself. He walked to the edge of the pine forest and followed the path around the banks of Lake Blitzen. The lake was so big and the water so pure and still, that it was a perfect mirror of the sky.

He travelled for days and nights. He spotted moose and, yes, on two occasions he did see more bears. Black bears. And once he had to climb a tree and wait an hour up in the branches for one of the bears to get bored and trudge away in the snow. He slept curled around the roots of trees, with Miika in his pocket or on the ground beside him. He lived on mushrooms and berries and fresh cool water.

He kept himself happy by singing Christmas tunes to himself, even though it was nowhere near Christmas, and weeing holes in the snow. He imagined being rich and waking up on

Christmas Day, having all the toys in the toyshop. Then he imagined something far better – giving his father a horse and cart.

But all the time, as he walked, it grew colder. Sometimes his feet hurt. Sometimes he went hungry, but he was determined to keep going.

He eventually passed through the village called Seipäjärvi that his father had told him about. It was just one street full of little wooden houses, painted red. He walked along the street.

An old toothless lady, bent double over a walking stick, was coming along the road. In

Nikolas's limited experience every village always had to have one old toothless person, walking around and saying scary things to strangers, so he was pleased that Seipäjärvi was no exception.

'Where go you, mysterious boy, with a mouse in your pocket?' she said.

'North,' is all he told her.

'To look for cheese,' added Miika, who still hadn't really got the point of the journey.

The old woman was quite weird, but not weird enough to understand mouse language, so she just looked at Nikolas and shook her head.

'Not north,' she said, her face as pale as a sheet. (A pale sheet, obviously.) 'Go east,' she said, 'or south, or west . . . Only a fool would go north. No one lives in Lapland. There is nothing there.'

'Well, I must be a fool,' said Nikolas.

'There is nothing wrong with being a fool,' said a Fool, with little bells on his shoes, who was passing by.

'The thing is, I'm looking for my father. He's a woodcutter. He's called Joel. He wears a red hat. He has very tired eyes. He only has nine and a half fingers. He was with six other men. They were on their way to the Far North.'

The old woman considered him. Her face creased like a map. And speaking of maps, she pulled out something crumpled in her pocket and handed it to him.

A map.

'There were some men, yes, now I think of it . . . Seven of them. They came through at the start of the summer. They had maps.' Nikolas felt a surge of excitement. 'They dropped this one.'

'Have they been back?'

The old lady shook her head. 'I tell you. Those that go north never return.'

'Well, thank you, thank you so much,' said Nikolas. He tried to smile to hide his worry. He had to give her something so he decided upon berries, as he didn't have much else. 'Please, please have these berries.' The old lady smiled in return and Nikolas saw her gums were brown and rotten.

'You are a good boy. Take my shawl. You'll need all the warmth you can get.'

And Nikolas, who could feel that even Miika, though relatively warm inside his coat pocket, was beginning to shiver, took the gift and thanked her again and went on his way.

ROUTE TO THE FAR NORTH

Lapland

The far North

Elghelm

Very large Mountain

Seipäjärvi

N

W   E

S

Kristinankaupunki

Turku

Helsinki

FINLAND

On and on he walked, following the map, over plains and ice-covered lakes and snow-covered fields and forests full of spruce trees.

One afternoon, Nikolas sat down underneath one of the snowy spruce trees and checked his feet. They were covered in blisters. The only bits of skin that weren't covered in blisters were bright red. And his shoes, which had been tatty to start off with, had practically fallen to pieces.

'It's no use,' he told Miika. 'I don't think I can go on. I'm too tired. It's getting too cold. I'll have to go home.'

But even when he said that word – '*home*' – he realised that he didn't have one. There was the cottage in the pine forest. But that wasn't home any more. Not with Aunt Carlotta living there. Not when he wasn't even able to sleep in his own bed.

'Listen, Miika,' he said, feeding the mouse a mushroom as he sat down by a tree. 'It might be best for you if you stayed in this forest. Look at the map. I don't know if we'll make it.'

Nikolas and Miika peered at the map, but the path they had to follow was illustrated by a dotted line that looked like footsteps in the snow. The map had no straight lines on it. It was just one long, curving path, weaving through forests and around lakes, towards a large mountain. He knew the mountain was large because it was called, on the map, 'Very Large Mountain'.

He lifted the mouse out of his pocket and placed him on the ground. 'Go on, Miika. Leave me. Look, there are leaves and berries. You'll be able to live here. Go. Go on.'

The mouse looked up at him. 'Leaves and berries? Don't insult me with talk of leaves and berries!'

'Seriously, Miika, it's for the best.' But Miika just crawled back onto Nikolas's foot, and Nikolas put the mouse back in his pocket. Nikolas rested his head on the mossy ground and pulled the old lady's shawl over him and right there, in daylight, he fell asleep.

As he slept, snow fell.

He had a dream, about being a child, and going to the hills near Lake Blitzen, and of being on the sleigh as his father pushed him and his mother laughed. He was so happy, inside that dream.

There was a scratchy feeling and he sprung

awake. Miika was pawing at his chest, and squeaking with fear.

'What is it, Miika?'

'I don't have a clue!' squeaked Miika. 'But it's really big, and it has horns on its head!'

Then Nikolas saw it.

The creature.

It was so close that for a moment he didn't know what it was. It certainly seemed large, from where Nikolas was sitting. But it wasn't a bear. It was covered in dark grey fur and had a broad strong-looking head. Like a moose, but definitely not one. The creature's chest was heaving with deep breaths, and wasn't grey, but as white as the snow. The animal was making strange noises, as if it was a pig crossed with a wolf. He saw the large velvet-haired antlers that bent and twisted like trees leaning in the wind.

Then he realised.

It was a reindeer.

A very big and very angry reindeer.

And it was staring straight at Nikolas.

The Reindeer

The reindeer stood back, looking large and ferocious. Its dark grey fur was the colour of the storm clouds above. It moved its giant head from left to right and then up, and let out a strange grunting roar, as a roll of thunder crashed in the sky.

Miika squeaked meekly in fear. Nikolas clambered to his feet.

'Good reindeer! Good boy! Good boy! Are you a boy?' (Nikolas looked.) 'You are a boy. It's all right. I'm not going to hurt you. Okay? I'm a friend.'

The words had no effect.

In fact they made the reindeer rear up on its hind legs. The animal towered above Nikolas, and its front hooves came within an inch from his face, pawing the air in anger.

Nikolas backed into a tree. His heart was pounding.

'What should we do?' he asked Miika, but

Miika clearly had no plans he felt inclined to share.

'Should we run?' Nikolas knew there was no way he would be able to outrun the reindeer. His breath whitened the air and he was rigid with shock.

The reindeer was a big heavy mass of muscle and fur and clouded nostril-breath. Through the stormy air he came, wild, grunting, huffing, with his head low now and the large antlers pointing directly into Nikolas's face. This must have been the largest and most furious reindeer in the whole of Finland.

Lightning flashed across the sky. Nikolas glanced up.

'Hold on tight, Miika,' Nikolas said, and he jumped up, grabbing the branch just above him with two hands, and swinging himself out of the reindeer's path as thunder rumbled. The reindeer collided straight into the spruce tree as Nikolas hooked his leg around the branch and held on even tighter. Nikolas was hoping that the reindeer would eventually get bored and leave him in peace, but the reindeer stayed there, pawing the ground and circling the tree.

Nikolas noticed something.

The reindeer was hobbling. There was a thin broken line of wood sticking out of one of its rear legs. It had been shot with an arrow.

Poor creature, thought Nikolas.

Just then, Nikolas felt the branch crack beneath him and he plummeted towards the snowy ground landing hard on his back.

'Aaagh!'

A shadow moved over him. It was the reindeer.

'Listen,' Nikolas gasped, 'I can get it out.'

He mimed the action of pulling an arrow out of a leg. Reindeer, as a rule, aren't very good at understanding mime, and so the reindeer swung his head around, his antlers crashing into Nikolas's ribs. This also caused Miika to fly out of his pocket, somersaulting through the air, only to collide with a tree.

Nikolas clambered to his feet, fighting off the pain.

'You're hurt. I can help you.'

The reindeer paused. It made a grunty, snuffling sound. Nikolas took a deep breath, summoned up all the courage he possessed, and edged forward. He gingerly touched the reindeer's leg, just above the arrow. He stopped.

The arrow feathers were grey. This was exactly like the arrow that had been fired at the bear. This was an arrow belonging to Anders the hunter.

'They've been here,' Nikolas thought aloud.

He scooped up some snow in his hands, remembering how his dad had once helped the moose. He padded snow around the wound, where the arrow was piercing the skin.

'This will hurt, okay? But afterwards you'll feel better.'

The arrow was stuck deep in the flesh, but Nikolas saw that the blood had hardened and realised that the arrow had probably been stuck there for days, if not weeks. The poor creature was moving again now, yanking his leg from left to right in pain. Then it made a deep anguished moan.

'It's all right. It's all right,' Nikolas said as he pulled the arrow out.

The reindeer shivered from the shock a little and turned, and bit Nikolas's thigh.

'Hey! I'm trying to help you.'

And then the reindeer bowed his head and stood still for a moment, and went to the toilet.

'Here,' said Nikolas, summoning up the last bit of courage he had. He scooped up some more snow and patted it on the wound.

After a couple of minutes the reindeer stopped shaking and seemed calmer. The clouds of air coming out of its nostrils grew smaller, and it started grazing in the snow looking for tufts of grass.

Sensing that the reindeer would finally leave him alone, Nikolas stood up on his aching blistered freezing feet, and brushed himself down. Miika ran over and Nikolas put him into his coat pocket. They both looked up and saw the largest brightest light in the night sky. The North Star. Nikolas checked around him, and saw a large lake to the east and ice plains to the west. He looked down at the map. They needed to walk directly north, in the straightest line possible. He started walking in that direction, crunching through the thickening snow. But after a little while he heard footsteps.

The reindeer.

Only this time it wasn't trying to charge him. It just tilted its head, like a dog might.

'I don't like that scary moose with trees growing out of his head,' grumbled Miika.

Nikolas carried on walking, and every time he stopped to look back, the reindeer stopped too.

'Shoo,' said Nikolas. 'You don't want to come with us, trust me. I still have a long way to go and I'm not much company.'

But the reindeer kept following him. Eventually, after several miles, Nikolas grew tired again. His legs felt heavy. He could see the soles of his feet through his shoes. And his head ached from cold and exhaustion. The reindeer though, despite his injured leg, didn't seem tired at all. Indeed, when Nikolas was forced to stop and rest his legs and take the pressure off his blisters the reindeer walked in front of him and, noticing Nikolas's damaged shoes and injured feet, lowered his head and knelt on his front two knees.

'You want me to climb on your back?' Nikolas asked.

The reindeer made a snuffling, grunting sort of sound.

'Is that "yes" in reindeer? Miika, what do you think?'

'I think "no",' said Miika.

Nikolas's legs were so tired and his feet so painful that he decided to risk it. 'You do realise there are two of us? My mouse and me. Is that okay?'

It appeared to be. So Nikolas climbed on the reindeer's back, and, well, did the only thing he could do.

He hoped for the best.

Something Red

As Nikolas discovered, riding a reindeer is a little easier than you think. It is a bit of a bumpy ride, but still a lot better than walking, especially walking on blistered feet. Indeed, even the bumpiness was something that Nikolas grew used to. He sat there, holding his hand delicately over his coat pocket to help keep Miika warm.

'I need to give you a name,' he told the reindeer. 'Names might not be important to reindeer but they are important to people. What about . . .' He closed his eyes and he remembered the dream he'd had, of sledging by Lake Blitzen, as a child. '*Blitzen*?'

The reindeer's ears pricked up, and he raised his head. Nikolas decided that Blitzen it should be. 'That's what I'm going to call you, if that's all right?'

And it seemed as if all was right.

Nikolas, Miika and Blitzen travelled together for what seemed like days. It got colder and colder, and Nikolas was thankful for having Blitzen, the old lady's shawl, and Miika to keep his hand warm in his pocket. He often leant forward to hug the reindeer and to feed him from the small supply of mushrooms and berries he kept in his right-hand pocket.

Eventually the landscape became entirely white, and Nikolas knew they were at the empty bit on the map. The snow got deeper and the wind got harsher, but Blitzen proved tough. His strong legs and sturdy frame powered through the deepening snow. It became difficult to see far ahead amid all the whiteness, but something was rising on the horizon. A vast wide craggy peak.

Finally, as the tiny sliver of a sickle moon hung low in the sky the snow stopped falling and they reached the Very Large Mountain.

Nikolas gave Blitzen his second to last mushroom, and his last one to Miika. He ate nothing himself, though his stomach rumbled like a distant storm. The mountain seemed to go on for ever. The further they climbed, the higher it seemed to get.

Blitzen was beginning to slow down, as if he finally was exhausted.

'Good boy, Blitzen,' Nikolas kept saying, wearily. 'Good boy.' He kept one hand over Miika to keep him safe in his pocket and occasionally used the other to pat the reindeer's back.

Blitzen's feet were pressing on nothing but snow now and it was getting thicker. It was a wonder he could keep going at all.

Nikolas felt blinded by the white until at

last, half way up the mountain, there was a flash of red, looking like a streak of blood, a scar in the snow. Nikolas jumped off the reindeer and clambered through the freezing whiteness towards it.

It was hard work. He sank into the snow, knee-deep every time he took a step. It was as if the mountain wasn't a mountain but just a giant pile of snow.

Eventually he got there. It wasn't blood though. It was a red hat and he recognised it in an instant.

It was his father's red hat.

The hat he had made from a red rag, and a fluffy white cotton bobble.

It was cold and frozen and clogged with powdery snow but there was no mistaking it.

Nikolas felt a deep, piercing anguish shoot through his weak body. He feared the worst had happened.

'Papa!' he shouted over and over again. He dug with his hands into the snow. 'Papa! Papa!'

He tried to tell himself that finding his father's hat didn't mean anything. Maybe it had just blown off his father's head and he had been in a hurry and hadn't been able to find it again. Maybe. But when your bones ache with cold and when you are starving with hunger, it is hard to keep looking on the bright side.

'Papa! Papaaaaa!'

He stayed there, digging the snow with his bare hands, until shaking and frozen he finally burst into tears.

'It's all useless!' Nikolas told Miika, who was looking out of his coat pocket, his small shivering head braving the cold. 'It's no use. He's probably dead. We must turn around.' He then shouted louder, addressing Blitzen. 'We must head south. I'm sorry. I should never have taken you with me. I shouldn't have taken either of you. It's too harsh and too dangerous, even for a reindeer. Let's go back where we came from.'

But Blitzen wasn't listening. He was walking away, struggling through the thick snow, climbing further up the mountain.

'Blitzen! You're going the wrong way! There's nothing for us there.'

But still Blitzen kept walking. He turned his head, as if to tell Nikolas to keep going. For a moment, Nikolas thought about staying still.

Just staying there until the snow covered him and until he was – like his father – part of the mountain itself. There seemed no point in going forwards or backwards. He realised how stupid he had been to leave the cottage. Hope finally left him.

It was so cold his tears froze on his face.

He knew it wouldn't take him long to die. Shivering, he watched Blitzen climb.

'Blitzen!'

He closed his eyes. He stopped crying. Waited for the chill to leave his bones and peace to come at last. But in a matter of minutes he felt a gentle, tender nudge against his ear. Opening his eyes he saw Blitzen's unblinking eyes behind a cloud of warm breath, looking at him in a way that made him think that he understood everything.

What was it that made Nikolas climb back on the reindeer?

Was it hope? Was it courage? Was it just a need to finish what he had started?

One thing is certain. Nikolas felt something beginning to burn inside him, weak and tired and cold and hungry and sad as he was. He grabbed hold of his father's hat, shook off the loose snow and put it on his head, and climbed back onto the reindeer. And the reindeer – tired and cold and hungry as *he* was – carried on walking up that mountain. Because that is what mountains are for.

The End of Magic

I f you keep on climbing a mountain you will eventually reach the top. That's the thing with mountains. However big they are, there is always a top. Even if it takes all through the day and all through another night you will usually get there, if you keep remembering there is a top. Well, unless the mountain is in the Himalayas, in which case the mountain just keeps on going and even though you know there is a top you freeze to death and all your toes fall off before you get there. But this wasn't *that* big a mountain. And Nikolas's toes didn't fall off.

He, Blitzen and Miika carried on, as green curtains of light filled the night sky.

'Look, Miika, it's the Northern Lights!'

And Miika stood on his hind legs in Nikolas's pocket, and stared up, and saw the vastness of the sky was filled with beautiful, mysterious, ghostly light. To be honest, Miika didn't care. Beauty is not of particular interest to a mouse, unless it was the beauty of the creamy yellowness or blue veins of a nice piece of cheese. So as soon as Miika peeked his head out of Nikolas's pocket he curled back down again.

'Isn't it wonderful?' said Nikolas, gazing up at the aurora, which looked to him like someone was sprinkling glowing green dust across the heavens.

'Warmth is wonderful,' said Miika.

By sunrise, they reached the top of the mountain. And though the sky was blue and the Northern Lights had disappeared, there was still glowing. Just lower down now, in the valley beyond the mountain. And this aurora wasn't just every variety of green, it was every colour in the rainbow. Nikolas looked at the map, trying to recognise any of the landscape. Beyond the mountain, the elf village was supposed to be there, visible, but there was nothing but a snow-filled plain of land leading towards the horizon. Actually, no. There were some hills in the distance, to the northwest, with tall pine trees, but there was no other sign of life.

They continued to head directly north, towards the multi-coloured lights, down the mountain, trudging through the light-filled air.

It was incredible how quickly Nikolas's spirits fell. On top of the mountain, everything had seemed possible, but now, trudging through thick snow, he was getting worried again.

'I must be going mad,' Nikolas said. His hunger was beginning to hurt, as though there was something alive, growling and moving, inside his stomach. He pulled his father's hat down over his ears. They walked on, through the snow, which was starting to thin a little, but still felt heavy, and through red and yellow and green and purple-tinged air. Also, Nikolas could sense that something was wrong with Blitzen. He was slowing down, and his head kept dropping so low Nikolas couldn't see his antlers.

'You need to sleep, I need to sleep,' said Nikolas. 'We've got to stop.'

But Blitzen didn't stop. He kept on. One faltering step after another until his knees buckled and he collapsed in the snow.

Thud.

Nikolas was trapped under him. And Blitzen, one of the largest reindeer there had ever been, was heavy. Miika crawled out of Nikolas's pocket and scampered over the snowy ground, round to Blitzen, scratching at his face to try and wake him.

'Blitzen! Wake up! You're on my leg!' shouted Nikolas.

But Blitzen wasn't waking up.

He could feel his leg was getting crushed. The pain throbbed, from his ankle through his entire body, until there was little else to think about. Just pain. He tried pushing against Blitzen's back, and wriggling his leg in the snow. If Nikolas hadn't been so weak and hungry he might have been able to free himself. But Blitzen was getting heavier and colder all the time.

'Blitzen!' yelled Nikolas. 'Blitzen!'

He realised he could just die here and no one would know or care. Terror filled Nikolas

with a new kind of chill, as the strange lights kept shifting in the air around him. Red, yellow, blue, green, purple.

'Miika, go . . . I think I'm stuck here . . . Go on . . . Go . . .'

Miika looked around, worried, but then saw something. Something Nikolas's human eyes couldn't see.

'What is it, Miika?'

Miika squeaked an answer that Nikolas couldn't understand.

'Cheese,' said Miika. 'I smell cheese!'

Of course, there was no cheese to be seen, but that didn't stop Miika. If you believed in something you didn't need to see it.

And so the mouse ran and kept running. The snow, though thick, was light and fluffy and evenly spread on the ground, and Miika was moving fast, churning through it, heading north.

Nikolas watched his mouse friend become a dot and then disappear completely. 'Goodbye, my friend. Good luck!'

He lifted his hand to wave. His fingers were so cold they had turned a deep, dark purple. It felt as if they were burning up. His stomach ached with cramp. His leg, squeezed between the weight of a reindeer and the weight of the world, was in agony. He closed his eyes, and imagined a vast feast. Ham, gingerbread, chocolate, cake, bilberry pie.

Nikolas lay back in the snow and felt an overwhelming exhaustion, as though life was leaving him too.

Miika had disappeared. And then Nikolas felt so dreadful he said something equally dreadful. The very worst thing that anyone can ever say. (Close your eyes and ears, especially if you are an elf.)

'There is no magic,' he whispered, delirious. And after that everything became darkness.

Father Topo and Little Noosh

There were voices in the dark . . .
'Kabeecha loska! Kabeecha tikki!' said
one voice. It was a strange voice.
Small, fast and high-pitched. A girl's
voice, maybe.

*'Ta huuure. Ahtauma loska es
nuoska, Noosh.'* This second voice
was slower and deeper, but still strange. It was
almost like singing.

Was he dead?

Well, no. Not quite. But nor was he alive,
and if they had found him and Blitzen even
just a minute later then they would have found
two dead bodies.

The first thing Nikolas noticed was the
warmth.

It felt like a kind of warm syrup was pouring
into him from the inside. He did not yet feel
the small hand pressed against his heart, but
he could still hear the voices, even if they did
sound a million miles away.

'What is it, Grandpapa?' said the high-pitched voice, which now – even more weirdly – Nikolas could understand perfectly, as if it was his own language.

'It's a boy, Noosh,' said the other.

'A boy? But he's taller than you, Grandpapa.'

'That's because he's a special kind of boy.'

'A special kind? What kind?'

'He's a human,' the deeper voice said, carefully.

There was a gasp. 'A *human?* Will he eat us?'

'No.'

'Should we run away?'

'It's perfectly safe, I'm sure. And even if it's not, we must never let fear be our guide.'

'Look at his weird ears.'

'Yes. Human ears can take a lot of getting used to.'

'But what about what happened to . . . ?'

'Come on, Little Noosh, we mustn't think of that. We must always help those who are in trouble . . . Even if they are human.'

'He looks terrible.'

'Yes. Yes, he does. That is why we must do everything we can, Noosh.'

'Is it working?'

'Yes.' A degree of worry rose up in his voice. 'I believe it is. And on the reindeer too.'

Blitzen woke and slowly rolled over, taking his weight off Nikolas, whose eyes were now blinking awake.

Nikolas gasped. For a moment he didn't know where he was. Then he saw the two creatures, and gasped again, because that is what you do if you see elves.

The elves were both quite short, as elves tend to be, although one was taller than the other. Nikolas could see the smaller one was a girl elf. She had black hair and skin whiter than the snow and sharp cheeks and pointed ears and large eyes slightly too far apart. She was wearing a dark green-brown tunic that didn't look very warm, but she didn't seem to be cold. The older and bigger elf was wearing a similar-coloured tunic and a red belt. He had a long white moustache and white hair and a serious, but kind look about him. His eyes twinkled like morning frost in sunshine.

'Who are you?' asked Nikolas. But really he meant *what* rather than *who*.

'I am Little Noosh,' said Little Noosh. 'What's your name?'

'I'm Nikolas.'

'And I am Father Topo, Noosh's grandpapa,' said the other elf, who was looking around him, to see if anyone was watching. 'Well, great-great-great-great-great-grandpapa, if we're being specific. We are elves.'

Elves.

'Am I dead?' asked Nikolas, which was a bit of a silly question, as for the first time in weeks he could feel warmth flooding through his veins and excitement rising in his chest.

'No. You are not dead,' said Father Topo. 'Despite your best efforts! You are very much alive, thanks to the goodness we found inside you.'

Nikolas was confused. 'But . . . but I don't feel cold. Or weak.'

'Grandpapa worked a little magic,' said Little Noosh.

'Magic?'

'A little drimwick.'

'Drimwick? What's that?'

Little Noosh looked at Nikolas and then at her grandpapa and back at Nikolas again. 'You don't know what a drimwick is?' she said.

Father Topo looked down at the little elf girl. 'He's from the other side of the mountain. There's not much magic where humans come from.' He smiled at Nikolas and Blitzen. 'A drimwick is a hope spell. You just close your eyes and wish for something, and if you wish in just the right kind of way you can make it happen. It's one of the earliest spells, laid out in the first *Book of Hope and Wonder.* That's an elf book about magic. I put my hand on you and your reindeer friend and I wished you to be warm, and to be strong, and to be always safe.'

'Always safe?' said Nikolas, confused, as Blitzen licked his ear. 'That's impossible.'

Little Noosh gasped as Father Topo covered her ears. 'Elves never ever say that word.' He shook his head. 'An impossibility is just a possibility you don't understand yet . . . but now, you must leave Elfhelm,' said Father Topo. 'And you must leave quickly.'

'Elfhelm? The elf village?' asked Nikolas. 'But I'm not even there.'

Little Noosh laughed a long elf laugh (which is very long indeed). Father Topo gave her a stern look.

'What's so funny?' asked Nikolas, thinking

that even if you had saved someone's life it was still rather rude to laugh at them.

'We are standing on the Street of Seven Curves,' giggled Little Noosh.

'What? This isn't a street. It's the middle of nowhere. There is just snow. And . . . sort of . . . colours.'

Little Noosh looked at Father Topo. 'Tell him, Grandpapa, tell him.'

Father Topo looked around to check no one was watching and quickly explained. 'This is the longest street in Elfhelm. We are in the southeastern corner of the village. The street winds westwards all the way to the Wooded Hills, beyond the fringes of the village.'

'Wooded Hills?' asked Nikolas. 'But I can't see anything. Just colours in the air.'

'And over there is Silver Lake and the Reindeer Field, and all the shops on Reindeer Field Street,' said Little Noosh, jumping up and down and pointing to the north.

'Lake? What lake?'

'And there's Elfhelm village hall,' she said, pointing in the opposite direction to nothing in particular.

Nikolas didn't understand. He stood up. 'What are you talking about?'

'Is he blind?' asked Little Noosh.

Father Topo looked at Nikolas then at Little Noosh. Very quietly he said, 'To see something, you have to believe in it. *Really* believe it. That's the first elf rule. You can't see something you don't believe in. Now try your hardest and see if you can see what you have been looking for.'

The Elf Village

Nikolas looked around him as, slowly, the hundreds of colours, floating in the air, became less ghostly and more real. More intense and vivid and solid. Nikolas watched as the colours that had before been floating as free as a gas in the air, formed themselves into lines and shapes. Squares, triangles, rectangles. Roads, buildings, a whole village, appearing out of the air. The elf village. They were standing on a street full of small green cabins. There was another road, a bigger one cutting into it from the east. Nikolas looked down at the ground. There was still snow. That hadn't changed. He cast his eyes along the wider road, heading north in front of him. On each side of the road stood buildings, timber-framed with snow-covered roofs. Nikolas saw that one of the buildings had a giant wooden clog hanging outside it. Another had a little spinning top painted onto a sign. A toy shop, maybe. Beyond that was the lake Little Noosh had told him about, like an oversized oval mirror, which was right next to a field full of reindeer. Blitzen had noticed this too, and was looking over with interest.

To the west, before the Wooded Hills, was a large round dark tower, pointing to the sky. Directly to the north was the place that Little Noosh had been pointing towards: Elfhelm village hall, made of dark, almost black timber. It was by far the largest building in the whole village. Not as tall as the tower (it was only two storeys high) but wide and with around twenty windows, which glowed with light. Nikolas could hear singing, and the smell of something sweet and wonderful was wafting from the direction of the hall. Something he hadn't smelt in over a year. Gingerbread. If anything, it smelt even better than it had done outside the baker's shop in Kristiinankaupunki.

'Wow, Elfhelm. My father was right, it's just how he described it.'

'I like your hat,' said Little Noosh.

'Thanks,' said Nikolas. He took the hat off and looked at it. 'It's my father's hat. He was on an expedition to Elfhelm. I wanted to know if he had made it. He was with six other men. He was called . . .'

But Little Noosh started excitedly talking over him. 'Red is my favourite colour! After green. And yellow. I like every colour, really. Except purple. Purple makes me feel sad thoughts. That is where we live,' she told him. She pointed towards a red and green cabin a small way in the distance.

'It's wonderful,' said Nikolas, 'but I also wondered if you'd seen a mouse?'

'Yes!' shouted Little Noosh. Father Topo quickly covered her mouth with his hand.

'Okay, human child, now you've seen Elfhelm, you had better take your reindeer and go,' said Father Topo. 'Whatever you expect to find, won't be here.'

Blitzen nudged Nikolas's shoulder as if he understood the new urgency in Father Topo's voice but Nikolas stayed where he was.

'I came to find my father,' he said. 'I've travelled over one thousand miles. Blitzen and I are not just going to turn around and go back.'

The old elf shook his head. 'I'm sorry. It's not wise for a human to be here. You must go back to the south. It's for your own good.'

Nikolas looked into Father Topo's eyes and

pleaded. 'My father is all I have got. I need to know if he made it to Elfhelm.'

'He could be our pet!' suggested Little Noosh.

Father Topo patted the elf girl on the head. 'I don't think humans like to be pets, Little Noosh.'

'Please, I come here peacefully. I just want to know what happened to my father.'

Father Topo considered. 'I suppose, given the season, there might be a chance you could be welcomed.'

This excited Little Noosh. 'Let's take him to the hall!'

'I won't cause any trouble. I promise,' said Nikolas.

Father Topo gave a quick glance over to the tall circular tower in the west. 'Trouble doesn't always have to be caused. It's sometimes already there.'

Nikolas had no idea what this meant, but he followed the elves, as they walked in their clogs towards the wooden hall beyond the lake. They walked onto the broad shopping street, passing a sign that declared simply 'The Main Path', and the clog-shop, and a bakery with smoke-stained windows, a toy-and-sleigh shop with a poster advertising lessons at the School of Sleighcraft.

He also passed a crooked black-tiled building, with windows made of ice. 'The Daily Snow' read the sign outside.

'The main elf newspaper,' explained Father Topo. 'Full of fear and nonsense.'

There were free copies of the newspaper piled high outside.

'LITTLE KIP STILL MISSING' was the headline, and Nikolas wondered who Little Kip was. He was about to ask, but though they were small, the elves were fast walkers and they were already some way ahead. He and Blitzen were struggling to keep up.

'What's that building?' he asked. 'The tall tower?'

'Look,' said Father Topo, changing the subject. 'That's the North Pole.' He pointed at a thin green rod sticking out of the ground.

Little Noosh spoke up. 'Do you think Father Vodol will be kind?'

'I think it will be all right,' said the old elf. 'Come on, Little Noosh. We elves are kind and welcoming in our hearts. Well, we always used to be. Even Father Vodol knows that . . .'

THIS SEASON'S LATEST CLOGS

PRICE 2 CHOCOLATE COINS

The Daily Snow

EVERY ELF'S FAVOURITE NEWSPAPER

LITTLE KIP STILL MISSING

If its not one thing its another, last yr it was the foods & then the reindeer, now it was jng flake maddott's on

Then the forest fading and now this. Little kid has been missing now for three weeks and its parents and family are devastated beyond anything as this is their own

And he was last seen in the little town roads and good with boomerin hats at near holiday, please help our a warm

REINDEER FLU HITS ELFHELM

It is not brother it another, its an illness last year all together like the same tradition before that there reindeer flu specialist doctor Rosal von Rosenberg has announced a cull on all reindeer infected stock.

Classified advertisements elf school exam results, up to date weather forecast.

PINE ROOTS CAUSE VILLAGE HALL MAYHEM

After three more weeks of underground discovery well pine growth begins to do at the root (no pun intended) of the village hall sewage problems. Elf build will be completing the necessary work out.

Nikolas was confused. 'Erm, Father Tippo?'

'Topo.' The old elf corrected him.

'Father Topo, sorry. I just wanted to ask if . . .'

'Here you are, Blitzen!' exclaimed Little Noosh.

They had reached the clear, icy lake. Just beyond it lay an open field where seven other reindeer were happily chewing lichen from the trees.

'Do you know if my father . . .'

Father Topo ignored him and called out to the reindeer. 'Oh, deerlings, come here! Here's a new friend.'

Meanwhile, Little Noosh was back to talking about her favourite colours. 'I quite like indigo. It's much nicer than purple. And crimson. And turquoise. And magenta.'

Blitzen stood behind Nikolas and nuzzled his shoulder. 'He's a bit anti-social,' Nikolas explained to Father Topo.

But one of the reindeer, a female, came over and gave Blitzen the gift of some grass. For a moment, Nikolas thought he saw her feet actually leave the ground – a gap between where the reindeer's body ended and where his shadow began. But maybe he had just imagined that.

'Ah, that's Donner,' said Little Noosh, 'the kindest of all.' Little Noosh started pointing at all the other reindeer. 'And there's Comet, with the white streak on his back, and Prancer, he's so funny, skipping with Cupid. Cupid will lick your hand off if you let him. Oh, and . . . and . . . and . . . the dark one, that's old Vixen, she's a bit of a grumpy thing, and that one is Dancer, and Dasher, who is the fastest of the lot.'

'Are you okay, boy?' Nikolas asked Blitzen, but Blitzen was already off, making friends. Nikolas noticed that the scar on Blitzen's leg had totally healed.

Once Blitzen was grazing contentedly, they walked on, past a sign pointing west to 'The Wooded Hills Where The Pixies Live'. The music got louder, the scent of gingerbread stronger, and a sense of fear mixed with a strange excitement until they had reached the door of the old village hall.

'Oh, and you do know what day it is, don't you?' said Father Topo, with a nervous smile.

'No. I don't even know the month!'

'It's the twenty-third of December! Two days till Christmas. This is our Christmas party. The only party we're allowed now. But not as good as it used to be, because dancing has been banned.'

Nikolas couldn't believe he had been away that long, but there were even harder things to believe, as he was about to find out.

The Mystery of Little Kip

If you were an eleven-year-old boy of sufficient height, like Nikolas, you would have to duck to get in through the Elfhelm village hall door. But once he was inside, Nikolas was overwhelmed by what he saw. There were seven extremely long wooden tables, around which were seated elves. Hundreds of elves. There were small elves and slightly less small elves. There were child elves and grown-up elves. Thin ones, fat ones, somewhere-in-between ones.

He had always imagined that seeing the elves would be the happiest thing in the world, but the atmosphere was very miserable. The elves were divided according to the colour of the tunic.

'I'm a green tunic,' said Father Topo. 'So that means we sit at the top table. The green tunics are members of the Elf Council. The blue tunics are the elves who have specialisms, like toymaking or sleighcraft or gingerbread making.

And the brown tunics are elves with no specialism. It didn't used to be like this. Before Father Vodol we all sat together. That was what being an elf meant. Togetherness.'

'Who is Father Vodol?'

'Sssh! Not so loud. He'll hear you.'

When Nikolas had imagined an elf Christmas, he had always thought there would be singing and that there would be lots of sweet things to eat. And there were sweet things to eat – the whole place smelt of cinnamon and gingerbread – though the elves didn't seem to be enjoying the food much. There was also singing, but the elves were singing it in the most miserable voices imaginable, despite the happy lyrics:

> *Our problems, well, they come and go,*
> *They fall and melt just like the snow.*
> *But so long as we can smile and sing,*
> *Problems they won't mean a thing.*
> *Because we can feast and we can rhyme,*
> *And be happy that it's Christmas time!*

But no one was happy. The faces were all sad, or sour. Nikolas felt uneasy. He whispered to Father Topo, 'What's the matter? Why do they look so unhappy?'

Before Topo could answer, his great-great-great-great-great-granddaughter proved that not *all* elves were unhappy. She was already squealing with joy: 'It's nearly *Christmas!*'

There was silence and a tightening of the air, as if the whole room was holding its breath. All the elves had noticed them now and turned to look at Nikolas.

Father Topo cleared his throat.

'Hello, elves! It looks like we have a special guest just in time for Christmas! Now, as it is Christmas time we should show kindness to others, and I think we should all show some good old-fashioned elf hospitality, even if he is a human.'

The elves gasped at the word.

'A human!' one cried. 'What about the New Rules?' This elf, who was wearing a blue tunic, had a strange beard. It was stripy. He was pointing to a poster, torn from the *Daily Snow*, that was pinned to the wall. It said: 'THE NEW RULES FOR ELVES'. And then gave a list.

Nikolas forced himself to smile and wave, but there was an awkward silence and only one small elf child waved back. Some of the old elves tutted and grumbled to themselves. It made no sense. Weren't elves meant to be

friendly? Every time Nikolas had pictured an elf he had pictured a happy creature, smiling, dancing, toymaking, and offering gifts of gingerbread. That was certainly what his father had told him. But maybe the stories weren't factually correct. These elves just turned and said nothing and gave very long glares. He had never considered glaring was such an important part of being an elf.

'Should I leave?' asked Nikolas, feeling uncomfortable.

'No. No, no, no. No. *No*,' said Little Noosh. And then, just to be clear: 'No.'

Father Topo shook his head. 'There's no need for that. You can sit down with us. We'll find some seats at the top table.'

The whole hall stayed quiet, listening to Father Topo's clogs tapping on the tiled floor as the three of them walked the length of the room. It was quite dark, with only five flaming torches on each wall, but Nikolas wished it were darker still, so that he couldn't be seen. Indeed, he wished he wasn't there at all, even though the food on each table was tantalising for a boy who had known nothing but mushrooms and the occasional cloudberry or lingonberry these past few weeks.

Gingerbread.

Sweet plum soup.

Jam pastries.

Bilberry pie.

Little Noosh held Nikolas's hand. Her hand was small, but her fingers were long and thin, with pointed little nails. She, like many young elves, knew goodness when she saw it. She had no doubt in her mind that, despite being human and having human ears, Nikolas wasn't somebody she should be afraid of. She led him to a seat. Half the elves at the table left in horror as they saw him approach, which meant there were now a lot of empty seats for him to choose from. He sat in the one right next to Little Noosh and as he did, the sight of so much delicious food made him momentarily forget all those elf eyes watching him and he picked up a bowl of plum soup from the middle of the table and drank it in one go, then he stuffed four jam pastries into his mouth, and had made a start on a slab of gingerbread before he noticed an elf woman opposite tutting at him.

The elf woman had bright blonde hair in two plaits that stuck out of the side of her head horizontally in perfect straight lines.

'We don't want your kind here,' she hissed. 'Not after last time.'

'But he's nice!' said Little Noosh. 'He wears a red hat. No one who wears a red hat can be a bad person! Red is the colour of life and love and sunsets.'

'Last time?' said Nikolas.

'Leave him alone, Mother Ri-Ri,' said Father Topo. 'He means no harm.'

'Harm? Harm? Harm! Of course he means *harm*. You ask Little Kip if he means no *harm* . . . He's human. Humans are all *harm*.'

Another elf – solemn-faced, at another table – piped up. 'Father Vodol won't be happy.'

Father Topo considered. 'That might be true, Father Dorin, but we are good elves.' He sighed.

Nikolas was confused.

'Who is Little Kip?' asked Nikolas, remembering the headline in the *Daily Snow*.

And as he said the words 'Little Kip' the other elves at the table stopped eating.

'It's probably best not to say anything,' shushed Father Topo.

'Can I just ask you one more thing?' said Nikolas.

'I'd just eat your food and then we should probably . . .'

Before Father Topo could finish his sentence another elf walked towards the table. This elf was the tallest of all the elves, but he was still only the same height as Nikolas was when he was sitting down. He had a long pointed nose, and a black beard that stretched almost to his knees, covering his tunic, and had the kind of screwed-up unpleasant face of someone heading into a permanently strong, icy wind. He was also holding a black wooden staff. All those elves that were still seated around the table looked away, or bowed their heads, or nervously played with their food.

'No more singing!' he said to the hall. 'Singing leads to merriment, and merriment leads to foolishness. I have told you. And this' – he was pointing at Nikolas – 'is why.'

Nikolas stopped eating too and met the stare of this scowling, black-bearded elf. His heart began to gallop, and a cold sense of dread fell over him.

THE NEW RULES FOR ELVES

1. Know your place.
2. Do not spickle dance.
3. Do not play with toys in public.
4. Do not play with spinning tops in private OR public.
5. Avoid joy and merriment at all times.
6. Worry more.
7. Resist goodwill.
8. Put your own interests before others.
9. Don't talk to pixies or trolls or other non-elves.
10. Never, under any circumstances, allow a human into Elfhelm.

An Unpleasant Encounter

h, Father Vodol!' said Father Topo. 'What a wonderful Christmas party. It is very good that you, as leader of the Elf Council, have made it so . . .'

'Never mind Christmas!' interrupted Father Vodol.

The hall fell into total silence. And then Father Vodol spoke again, with quiet menace. 'Father Topo, I need to speak with you, and the human. In the Council Room. Now.'

'The Council Room?'

The elf raised his staff and pointed towards the stairs. 'Now, Father Topo. No delay. Quick as a reindeer.'

Father Topo nodded. He turned and told Little Noosh to wait there and beckoned for Nikolas to follow him. Nikolas did as he was told but felt a little ridiculous at having to duck as he climbed up the stairs at the back of the hall, up to a floor with a very low ceiling, with even lower timber beams.

Nikolas followed the elves past two others in black clothes. These were male elves but had no beards. They were guarding a door that said 'Council Room'. Then Nikolas found himself in a room that he was a bit too tall for. There was a long table with twenty chairs around it. Each of the chairs had a name engraved into it.

'Shut the door!' said Father Vodol, before addressing Father Topo.

'Were you not at the last meeting, Father Topo?' he asked, pointing to the chair with Father Topo's name engraved on it.

'Yes, yes, I was.'

'So you will know about the new rules for elves. No humans must be brought here.'

'Well, I didn't bring him here. I found him. Him and his collapsed reindeer. A whisker from death, so I . . . so I . . .' As Father Topo became nervous, Father Vodol stared intently at the elf's clogs. Within a second, the white-haired elf was off his feet, floating in the air.

'So you *what*?' asked Father Vodol. Nikolas noticed Father Topo was now gasping for air, even though Father Vodol was nowhere near him. Father Topo had tipped upside down and was now rising towards the ceiling, with nothing holding onto him. Biscuits fell out of his pocket. His moustache drooped beside his nose.

'Please,' Nikolas said. 'It's not his fault. He was only trying to . . .' And then Nikolas stopped speaking, because his mouth was closed shut. He couldn't move his lips or his jaw. Father Vodol might have been short but his magic was strong.

'I did a little hope spell,' spluttered Father Topo.

Father Vodol's brow reddened with anger. 'A drimwick? On a human?'

The upside-down elf nodded. 'Yes, Father Vodol. I'm sorry. But it was the only way I could save him. And drimwick only works on the good, so I thought it safe. And I was with Little Noosh. What kind of example would it have set if I had let him die right there in front of her?'

Father Vodol quivered with rage. 'Do you know what this means?! You do know that you have given the human gifts he should not have. I take it you have told Little Noosh what happened to Little Kip!'

Nikolas tried to speak, but his jaw was still locked, and his tongue lay as still as a dead fish inside his mouth.

'No. I don't want to scare her. I want her to believe the best in people. Even human people. She sees the good in . . .'

Father Vodol's skin above his beard grew redder and redder, like a sun setting over a thorn bush. Furniture shook, as though the whole room was sharing Father Vodol's fury. 'Our powers are *not* for humans.'

'Please,' begged Father Topo. 'Let us remember how things used to be. Before . . . We are elves. We use our powers for good. You remember. When your newspaper was full of only good news?'

Father Vodol laughed. 'It's true. The *Daily Snow* used to be full of good news. But good news doesn't sell newspapers.'

'But good is good!'

Father Vodol nodded. 'I do not disagree, Father Topo. We must indeed use our powers for good. Which is why we must send a clear message that no outsiders are allowed here any more. We must have strength of purpose and unity. It's lucky for our community that nobody here has a stronger will than the Holder of the Staff, which is me. I was elected, in a democratic fashion, to rule Elfhelm as I see fit.'

Father Topo, still struggling in the air, gasped, 'In fairness, Father Vodol, it did help that you owned the *Daily Snow*, and had the newspaper to support your election.'

'Get out!' said Father Vodol.

As though by force of will Father Vodol threw poor old Father Topo right out of the window. Nikolas heard a splash and ran to see the elf had landed in the lake outside the building. He tried to shout to see if his new friend was okay but his mouth was still firmly locked.

'Now, human, tell me why you came here,' said Father Vodol.

Nikolas turned back towards the furious black-bearded elf. He felt his jaw warm and soften and unlock. His tongue came to life again. 'I wanted to go to the Far North. I wanted to find . . .'

'What?' Father Vodol put a hand in his pocket and pulled out a mouse. 'This mouse?'

Miika looked at Nikolas, terrified.

'Miika, are you okay?'

'Don't worry, mice are welcome here. Mice have never done us any harm . . .'

Father Vodol gave a small squeal of pain. Miika had bit him.

Then he jumped out of Father Vodol's hand and scurried over to Nikolas. Nikolas picked Miika up and put him safely in his pocket.

'So, you have what you came for. Now go. Get out of my sight.'

'No. Not totally. I set out to find my father,' Nikolas said.

The elf's eyes widened. 'So why did you think he was here?' he asked darkly.

'Because he was going to the Far North. He always told me you were real. Elves, I mean. And he believed in you. And I tried to believe in you too. Anyway, he was heading here, with some others, to find proof that you exist . . .' Nikolas heard his own voice crack. He could crumble, just like gingerbread. 'But I don't know if he ever made it here.'

The elf stroked his beard. 'Hmmm. Interesting.' His voice was softer now. He broke off a corner of the roof on a gingerbread house that was in the middle of the table and ate a bit of it. He came closer. He even gave a curious smile. 'Describe your father. What did he look like?'

'He is tall. Nearly twice as tall as me. And he is strong, because he is a woodcutter. And he has colourful clothes that are a bit tatty, and a sleigh and an axe and . . . '

Father Vodol's eyes widened. 'Tell me, out of curiosity, how many fingers does your father have?'

'Nine and a half,' answered Nikolas.

Father Vodol smiled.

'Have you seen him? Is he still alive?' asked Nikolas, desperately.

Father Vodol raised the hand holding the staff. Nikolas saw the table rise off the ground, along with the chairs, only to slam down and break through the floor, falling into the dining hall below, where the elves were still eating their Christmas feast. The table and chair narrowly missed hitting anyone and smashed onto the floor below.

The elves all gasped and could see Nikolas and Father Vodol – who was now raising his voice for all to hear – still standing in the Council Room.

'So let me get this right. YOUR FATHER IS JOEL THE WOODCUTTER?'

Nikolas had nothing but the truth. 'Yes.'

The elves downstairs gasped again, only louder, and all started talking.

'His father is Joel the Woodcutter!'

'His father is Joel the Woodcutter!'

'His father is Joel the Woodcutter!'

For a moment, Nikolas forgot whatever trouble he might be in. 'My father made it here? He actually made it to the Far North? To Elfhelm? Did you meet him? Is he . . . is he still here?'

Father Vodol walked around the hole he had made in the floor and came close enough for Nikolas to smell the liquorice on his breath and to see a long thin scar beneath his beard. 'Oh, he came here all right. He was one of them.'

'What do you mean, one of them? What did you do to him?'

Father Vodol inhaled deeply. He closed his eyes. His forehead bubbled and rippled like water in the wind. And then he did one of his favourite things. He did a Big Speech. And this is how it went:

'Oh, I did something,' he said. 'I *trusted* him. That was my greatest mistake as leader of the Elf Council. I listened to the goodwill of the elves who live here. But I kind of knew all along that goodwill is just another name for weakness. And goodwill comes from happiness, so I have tried very hard these last few weeks to increase unhappiness. Unhappiness is severely underrated, especially with elves. For one thousand years, elves had been happy and joyful. They made gifts for visitors who never came here. They even built a Welcome Tower. What fools we've been! And every Tuesday, whoever was leader of the Council would sit down and talk about Welcoming Strategies. THERE WAS NO ONE TO WELCOME!'

He paused for a moment. Pointed to one of several elf portraits on the wall. A painting of an elf with a large golden bun of hair on top of her head, and a very large and kind smile.

'Mother Ivy,' he said. 'She was the leader of the Elf Council before me. She'd been leader for one hundred and seven years. Her slogan was "Joy and Goodwill for All"! It disgusted me. And not just me . . . Increasingly, over the years, elves began to realise it was wrong to live for other people. So, I put myself forward for election. "Elves for Elves". That was my motto. And I got in. Easy peasy. Mother Ivy wished me well, of course, and gave me a fruitcake and made me some fleece stockings. I gave her a role as Forest Troll Peace Envoy and she was eaten within a week. They ate all of her except her left foot, because of some pretty bad bunions. With hindsight, I think she was probably the wrong person for the job. Bit too friendly.'

He sighed a long sigh, as he gazed up at the portrait.

'Poor Mother Ivy. But the trouble is, she didn't understand that other creatures are not like us. You see, in their heart elves know that they are the best of all species. They just needed someone to stand up and tell them.

'But I couldn't go the whole hog. Not until Little Kip was kidnapped. After that, I changed things, and changed them quickly. I instantly tried to make elves more miserable, for their own good. I made them wear different-coloured tunics, and sit at separate tables. I banned spickle dancing, lowered the minimum wage to three chocolate coins a week, and stopped the unsupervised use of spinning tops. I spent every day trying to find the scariest headlines for my newspaper, the *Daily Snow*. I even changed Mother Ivy's slogan to "Tough

on Goodwill, Tough on the Causes of Goodwill". I was proud of that.' He glared at Nikolas as his smile curled like a cat's tail. 'And the very first thing I did was to ban outsiders and to change the Welcome Tower into a prison . . . Guards!' he shouted. 'Take the human to the tower!'

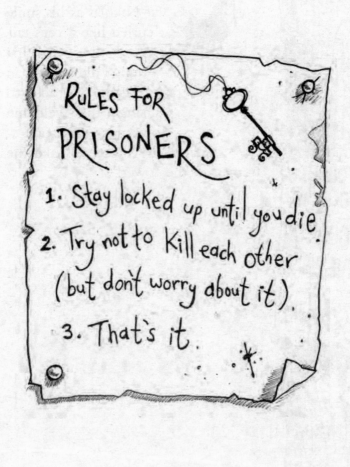

The Troll and the Truth Pixie

Nikolas had seen the tower. It was the tall thin round building to the west of the village. It seemed to get taller as the guards pushed him closer, along the path through the snow. He could feel Miika, trembling against his chest. 'This is all my fault,' whispered Nikolas. 'You must escape. Look. There. Those hills over there with the trees, behind the tower. Run to them. Hide. You'll be safe there.'

And Miika looked and smelt the air and he noticed that the air from that direction smelt faintly delicious – faintly cheese-like.

The elf guard who was nearest to them pointed his little axe up towards the boy. 'Stop talking!'

As the two guards looked away Nikolas took Miika out of his pocket and placed him on the ground. 'Go, Miika. Now!' The little creature sprinted away towards the Wooded Hills and the pretty little yellow cheese-scented cottages.

'Hey,' said a guard, beginning to chase after the rodent.

'Leave it!' ordered Father Vodol. 'We can lose a mouse, but not a human.'

'Goodbye, my friend.'

'Silence!' barked Father Vodol. And this time it was fear rather than magic that caused Nikolas to keep his mouth shut. Nikolas had never felt so alone.

The tower – the prison – was a scary place. Yet, although it was horrid, it also had very nice comforting things written on the stone walls of the staircase, from its time as the Welcome Tower. Things like 'Welcome' and 'Strangers are just friends with weird faces' and 'Hug a human'.

One of the blue tunic-wearing elf guards saw Nikolas reading these signs.

'Back in Mother Ivy's time I would have been obliged to cook you gingerbread and show you my spickle dancing, and yet now I have permission to chop you up into little pieces. I cry myself to sleep every night, and feel dead inside, but society is definitely improving.'

'I quite like the sound of your old society.'

'It was a mistake. It was full of friendliness and happiness and dancing. Not important things like fear and disliking outsiders. Father Vodol has made us see the error of our ways.'

After a long climb up a winding dark staircase Nikolas was thrown into the cell right at the top. Unfortunately, the tower was made of stone, not wood. It had no windows and its walls were streaked charcoal-black. The tiny glow from a flaming torch on the wall helped Nikolas's eyes adjust to the light. Someone ginormous was snoring under a blanket on a tiny bed, and out of the corner of his eye Nikolas could see a small black hole in the centre of the ceiling. The guards slammed the door closed and the loud reverberating echo trembled through Nikolas like dread.

'Hey! Let me out! I've done nothing wrong!' Nikolas shouted.

'Sssh!' came a voice, causing Nikolas to jump. He turned, and there, veiled in flickering shadow, was a sprightly-looking creature wearing yellow clothes and an innocent smile. This creature was no more than a metre tall, she had pointed ears and long hair and an angelic little face that looked as pure and delicate as a snowflake, though her cheeks were a bit grubby.

'Are you an elf?' he whispered, but already doubting the idea.

'No. I'm a pixie. A Truth Pixie.'

'A Truth Pixie? What's one of them?'

'One of them is me. But be quiet or you'll wake Sebastian.'

'Who's Sebastian?'

'The troll,' she said, pointing her pale pixie finger towards the large misshapen creature that was currently scratching his backside as he dozed on the tiny bed.

Sebastian seemed a peculiar name for a troll, but Nikolas didn't comment. He was too worried that he would never be able to escape this damp cold mouldy room.

'When do they let us out of here?' Nikolas asked the pixie.

'Never,' said the Truth Pixie.

'You're lying!'

'I can't lie. I'm a Truth Pixie. I have to tell the truth. That's what gets me into trouble. Well, that and making people's heads explode.'

She quickly covered her mouth with her

hand, ashamed of the words she had just blurted out.

Nikolas looked at her. He couldn't imagine anyone who looked less likely to hurt anyone.

'What do you mean, explode their heads?'

She tried to stop herself but couldn't help pulling a small golden leaf from her pocket. 'Hewlip.'

'Hewlip?'

'Yes. I gave an elf some hewlip soup and their head exploded. It was so much fun it was almost worth life imprisonment. I am saving my last leaf for someone special. I love seeing heads explode. I can't help it!'

Nikolas felt fear prickle his skin. If even the sweetest-looking pixie could turn out to be a murderer, there really was no hope.

'Would you like to see my head explode?' Nikolas asked, although he was petrified of the answer.

The Truth Pixie desperately tried to lie. 'Nnnnnnnnnnn . . . *yes*! I would like that so much!' Then she looked guilty. 'Sorry,' she added, softly.

Worried that the Truth Pixie might try to put hewlip in his mouth as he slept Nikolas vowed to himself that he would do everything in his power to stay awake for as long as possible, indeed for ever if need be.

The troll rolled over in bed and opened his eyes.

'What be you?' asked the troll, and though he was big, he wasn't slow, and a moment later Nikolas was struggling for breath as a rough-textured warty hand grabbed him by the throat and squeezed hard.

'I be . . . I . . . I *am* Nikolas. A boy. A human.'

'A hu–man? What be a hu–man?'

Nikolas tried to explain but he couldn't breathe and all that came out was a strangulated gurgle.

'Humans live beyond the mountain,' explained the Truth Pixie. 'They come from the south. They are very dangerous. Squeeze his neck until his head falls off.'

Nikolas looked at the Truth Pixie, who smiled sweetly.

'Sorry,' she said. 'I just can't help it.'

The troll thought about killing Nikolas but decided against it. 'It be Christmas Day,' he said to himself. 'Bad luck to kill on Christmas Day.'

'It's the twenty-third of December,' said the Truth Pixie, helpfully. 'If you want to kill him, I suggest you go ahead.'

'That be Troll Christmas Day. Troll Christmas come early. Can't kill on Christmas Day . . .' He let go of Nikolas's neck.

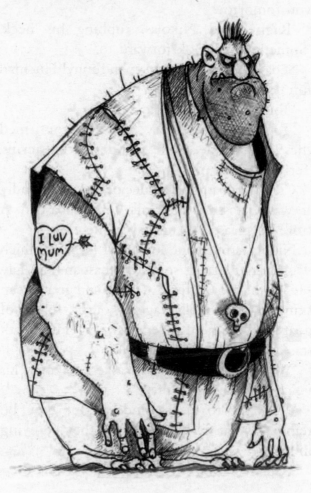

'That's ridiculous,' sighed the Truth Pixie. 'Christmas Day is the twenty-fifth of December.'

Sebastian stared down at Nikolas. 'I be kill you tomorrow.'

'Right,' said Nikolas, rubbing his neck. 'Something to look forward to.'

Sebastian laughed. 'Hu-man funny! Hu-man funny! Like Tomtegubb!'

'Tomte . . . what?' said Nikolas.

'Tomtegubbs are very amusing,' confirmed the Truth Pixie.' And wonderful musicians. Terrible cooks, though.'

Clearly Sebastian had decided to be friendly. It was Christmas after all. 'I be Sebastian. A troll. Be pleased to meet you, hu-man!'

Nikolas smiled and looked at his face, which was trickier than it sounds. Sebastian was ugly. He had only one (yellow) tooth and grey-green skin and a smelly ragged outfit made of goatskin. And he was very, very big. His breath stank of rotten cabbage.

'Why are you in here?' asked Nikolas, his voice trembling with fear.

'I be try to steal reindeer. But they be reindeer what fly like bird. And they be flying in sky.'

'Reindeer don't fly,' said Nikolas but even

as he said it he remembered Donner trotting off the ground and detaching from her shadow in the Reindeer Field.

'Of course elves' reindeer can fly,' pointed out the Truth Pixie. 'They've been drimwicked.'

'Drimwicked?' Nikolas remembered. *Drimwick*. That was the word that Father Topo and Little Noosh had used to bring him and Blitzen back to life. It was a magical word. Just to say it out loud was to feel a little warmer, as if your brain was coated in sun-warmed honey.

'A drimwick is a hope spell. If you have been drimwicked it gives you powers, even if you are only a reindeer,' said the Truth Pixie.

'What kind of powers?'

'It takes all that is good in you, and makes it stronger. It makes it magical. If you wish for something good, the magic will help. It is a very *boring* kind of magic. Because being good is very boring.'

Nikolas thought about Aunt Carlotta throwing Miika out of the door. 'No,' he told the grubby-faced pixie. 'You're wrong. The whole world – or the world I come from, the world of the humans, is full of bad things. There's misery and greed and sadness and hunger and unkindness all over the place. There are many,

many children who never get any presents, and who are lucky to get anything more than just a few spoonfuls of mushroom soup for dinner. They have no toys to play with and they will go to bed hungry. Children who don't have parents. Children who have to live with horrible people like my Aunt Carlotta. In a world like that it's very easy to be bad. So when someone is good, or kind, it's a magic in itself. It gives people hope. And hope is the most wonderful thing there is.'

Sebastian and the Truth Pixie listened to this in silence. The troll even shed a tear, a tear that rolled down his crumpled grey face and fell on the dusty stone floor and turned into a little pebble.

'I wish I was good,' said the Truth Pixie, looking down sadly at her hewlip leaf. 'If I was good I could be at home right now, eating cinnamon cake.'

'I glad I be troll and not hu-man,' said Sebastian, shaking his head and sighing. ''Specially you. 'Cause you be dead tomorrow.'

The Scariest Thought

Nikolas tried to ignore the threat of death, and the troll's giant grey, warty neck-strangling hands, and turned again to the Truth Pixie. He was still a bit frightened of her, but knew that being frightened wasn't a very useful thing to feel. He also knew that if he wanted answers there had to be no better place than this particular prison cell. 'If I ask you questions do you have to tell me the truth?'

She nodded emphatically. 'Yes, I'm a Truth Pixie.'

'Of course. Good. Right. Okay. So, let me think . . . Do you know if my father's alive? He's a human – obviously – and he's called Joel.'

'Joel who?'

'Joel the Woodcutter.'

'Hmmm. Joel the Woodcutter. It doesn't ring any bells,' said the Truth Pixie.

'What about Little Kip?'

'Little Kip! Yes. The little elf boy. I've heard of him. He was on the front page of the *Daily Snow*. It's an elf newspaper, but some of us pixies over in the Wooded Hills like to read it, just in case we read about any elves that have eaten hewlip and exploded. Oh, and for the recipes. And the gossip.'

'Did Little Kip's head explode?' Nikolas asked.

'Oh no. He was kidnapped.'

'Kidnapped?'

'And not by pixies or trolls either. I don't think it would have been such a big deal if it had been pixies or trolls or even a Tomtegubb. But no. He was kidnapped by humans.'

Nikolas felt a sudden chill. 'Which humans?'

'I don't know. A group of men. Forty-one moons ago. They came here and everyone eagerly welcomed them. Vodol ordered a special feast in the village hall in their honour and they were invited to stay for as long as they wanted, but in the middle of the night they kidnapped an elf child, and they led it away on a sleigh and escaped before the sun rose.'

Nikolas's heart skipped a beat. 'A sleigh?'

He felt properly terrified now. It was like

falling while staying still. He took his father's hat off his head and stared at it. Even scarier than the thought of being killed by a troll, even scarier than being locked in an elf prison, was the idea that his own father could have been one of the men who had kidnapped Little Kip. He didn't want to say this out loud, but it was a truth in his mind now, and he wanted to make it right.

He wanted to make *everything* right.

Nikolas looked up at the tiny dark hole. 'Truth Pixie, do you know what that hole is in the ceiling?'

'Yes, I do. You see, this didn't used to be a prison. This used to be a Welcome Tower, back when Mother Ivy was in charge.'

'I know. Father Vodol told me.'

'Elves were always welcoming creatures. This place used to be full of friendly elves giving out free plum wine to everyone who came here. Which was no one, but the thought was there. This room was the furnace. They used to have a fire here, which could be seen for miles around, so that those visitors who believed in elves and pixies and magic could find their way here.'

'I like smoke,' added Sebastian, thoughtfully.

'And so that hole you see in the ceiling . . .' said the Truth Pixie.

'Was the chimney?' asked Nikolas.

'Precisely.'

Nikolas stared up at the dark hole. If he put an arm above his head and jumped up he could probably reach in and touch the sides. But it was impossible to escape. The chimney was smaller than him. Even the Truth Pixie wouldn't be able to squeeze inside.

But then, what had Father Topo said to him?

'An impossibility is just a possibility that you don't understand,' he said, out loud.

'Yes,' said the Truth Pixie. 'That is the *truth*.'

The Art of Climbing
Through Chimneys

Sebastian fell back to his snoring. The sound was like a motorbike, but motorbikes hadn't been invented yet, so Nikolas couldn't compare it to that. Then soon after, the Truth Pixie fell asleep too. The troll was still hogging the bed, so the Truth Pixie had curled up on the floor, holding onto her hewlip leaf. Nikolas was extremely tired. He had never felt so tired before. Not even before Christmas, when he was never able to sleep because he was so excited. He knew he needed to sleep, but he didn't trust the Truth Pixie. He sat with his back against the cold hard wall staring up at the chimney. Outside, beyond the thick wooden door, in-between Sebastian's snores, he could just about hear the mumbled voices of the elf guards.

He had to get out of here. Not simply because he was with two creatures who, each for different reasons, wanted to kill him. No. He had to escape and find his father. He had a hunch that he was still alive and he also knew that he was probably with the men who were supposed to have taken Little Kip. There must be some confusion. His father was a good man.

He had to find him.

He had to bring back Little Kip.

He had to make everything all right. But how?

He remembered the day his mother died. Hiding from the brown bear, in the well, holding onto the chain holding the bucket, then losing her grip. The wail, as she fell, while Nikolas watched in horror from the cottage.

On that day, and for a lot of days after (let's say one thousand and ninety-eight) he had believed that things could only get worse and that he would wake up in tears for the rest of his life, feeling guilty that he hadn't stayed with her, even though he thought she was running too.

He prayed, somehow, for her to come back.

Joel kept on telling him he looked like his mother but his cheeks weren't as red so sometimes Nikolas used to grab some berries and crush them on his cheeks and look at his reflection in the lake. And in the blurry water he could almost imagine it was her, looking back from a dream.

'It's funny, Papa,' he once said, as his father chopped a tree. 'But I could probably have filled that well with tears the amount I have cried.'

'She wouldn't want you to cry. She'd want you to be happy. Jolly. She was the happiest person I ever met.'

And so the next morning Nikolas woke up and didn't cry. He was determined not to. And nor had he had his usual nightmare about his mother falling, falling, falling down that well. So he knew that terrible things – even the *most* terrible things – couldn't stop the world from turning. Life went on. And he made a promise to himself that, when he grew older, he'd try and be like his mother. Colourful and happy and kind and full of joy.

That was how he was going to keep her alive.

There were no windows in the tower.

The door was thick wood and solid metal. And besides, there were the guards. He was there, in this damp stone circular room, as stuck as an axle in a wheel. There was a world out there, a world of forests and lakes and mountains and hope, but that world belonged to other people now. Not him. There simply was no way out. And yet, strangely, he wasn't unhappy. Scared, yes, maybe a little, but also, deep down, hopeful. He began to chuckle to himself.

Impossible.

That was what Father Topo had meant, he realised.

That was the point of magic, wasn't it? To do the impossible.

Could he – Nikolas – really do magic?

He stared at the chimney, at the small circle of darkness. And he tried to concentrate hard on that chimney, that dark tunnel, and how to get through it. It was an intense darkness, like the darkness of the well. He thought of his mum, falling, and all those times he had imagined it the other way. Of her rising back into life. He thought of staring at the brown bear in the forest that last time, not really that scared, and the bear going away.

His head kept on saying it was impossible but he stared and stared and, slowly, he started to hope. To wish. He thought of all those unhappy elves in the hall. He thought of his father's sad face the day he had left the cottage to travel north. He thought of Aunt Carlotta making him sleep outside in the cold. He thought of human unhappiness. But he also thought of how it didn't need to be like that. He thought that, really, humans and probably even elves were good inside but had lost their way a bit. But most of all, he thought of how he could escape the tower.

And then he thought of his mother, smiling and laughing and being happy, no matter what.

He began to feel the same peculiar feeling, as if a warm syrup was pouring inside him, just as he had when he first met Father Topo and Little Noosh. It was a feeling of unbreakable joy. Hope, where no hope could exist. And then, before he knew it, he was rising. He was floating off the ground, and very slowly and surely he was climbing through the air above the Truth Pixie and Sebastian. He felt as light as a feather, until he hit his head against the ceiling, right next to the too-small black chimney flue. He fell back towards the ground, but landed on top of Sebastian.

'It not be Christmas Day now. It be the day after Christmas Day,' said Sebastian, as he woke up. 'So I be killing you.'

Amid the commotion, the Truth Pixie had woken up. 'Yay!' squealed the Truth Pixie. 'I mean, it's technically Christmas Eve. But otherwise – yay!'

Nikolas moved fast, and grabbed the yellow hewlip leaf from the Truth Pixie's hand. He thrust the leaf towards Sebastian, but it wasn't the leaf that caused the one-toothed troll to step backwards. It was the fact that Nikolas was suspended in the air again.

'You be magic. Why you be staying here if you be magic?'

'I'm beginning to ask myself the same thing,' said Nikolas.

'Hey!' said the Truth Pixie. 'Get down now and give me my leaf back.'

'Get away from me,' said Nikolas, trying to sound as fearsome as he could.

'Hmmm, that's tricky actually, as we are trapped in a *prison cell*,' said the Truth Pixie.

Sebastian grabbed Nikolas's leg and tried to pull him back down to the ground.

'Oh, this is so exciting,' said the Truth Pixie, smiling broadly and clapping her hands. 'I love a drama!'

Sebastian's grip tightened, his rough hands as strong as stone.

'Get . . . off,' said Nikolas, but it was no use. He thought of his mother falling, not rising, and that – combined with the strength of the troll – was interfering with the magic. Then something rough was around Nikolas's neck squeezing hard. Sebastian's free hand. Nikolas gasped.

'I . . . can't . . . breathe . . .'

Then the hand released.

'I be thinking,' said Sebastian, matter-of-factly. 'I might be eating you instead of strangling. I be only have one tooth but it be doing the job.'

And he opened his mouth and was about to bite, when Nikolas shoved the hewlip leaf in his mouth. The Truth Pixie clapped her hands in excitement.

'Hey!' came a deep elf voice from outside the door. 'What's going on in there?'

'Nothing!' said Nikolas.

'Nothing!' said Sebastian.

The Truth Pixie covered her mouth but still

couldn't help herself. 'The human boy is floating in the air while Sebastian is trying to eat him but now the human boy has shoved a hewlip leaf into his mouth so I am anxiously awaiting the explosion of Sebastian's head,' she blurted out.

'Emergency!' shouted the elf guard behind the door. 'There's a crisis in the furnace room!'

Sebastian stumbled backwards as the clop of elf footsteps could be heard echoing up through the tower's spiral staircase. Then the troll's face began to tremble. Sebastian looked worried.

'What be happening?'

Nikolas heard the troll's stomach rumble. It was more than a rumble. It was more, even, than a grumble.

It sounded like thunder.

Nikolas was now back on the floor.

'I'm sorry,' said Nikolas.

'He's gonna blow!' squealed the Truth Pixie. 'A Christmas Eve spectacular!'

The more-than-grumbling noise rose higher inside the troll, and now the noise was coming from his head. His cheeks wobbled. His forehead started to throb. His lips started to swell. His ears bulged. His head had already been big but it was getting bigger and bigger, it was now wider than his shoulders and he was struggling to hold it up, and all the time the Truth Pixie was clapping her hands in excitement.

'This is going to be a good one. I can feel it!'

The guards were at the door, trying to find the right key.

Sebastian tried to speak but he couldn't because his tongue was now the size of a slipper. 'Buh-buh-buhbuhbuh-buh-burbubbur,' he said, as he clutched his head. His eyes were now so large that they nearly popped out of his head. Well, one *did* pop out, and it rolled along the floor towards Nikolas. It lay there, looking up at Nikolas, and was pretty disgusting.

And the Truth Pixie burst into hysterics, looking at the eye. 'This is so good. Shouldn't laugh. Bad Pixie. Bad. But it's just so . . .'

Nikolas saw the Truth Pixie's face go still. 'What's up?' he asked.

'I just wet myself,' she said, and then she started giggling again.

150

'What's happening in there?' shouted the guards.

'I wouldn't open the door just yet,' said the Truth Pixie. 'There's going to be an explo–!'

And that was the moment Sebastian's head got so big that it exploded, with a loud wet thud. Purple troll blood and grey troll brains splattered everywhere. Over the walls and the Truth Pixie and Nikolas.

'A-ma-zing!' said the Truth Pixie, as she applauded. 'Bravo, Sebastian!'

Sebastian didn't respond to the Truth Pixie. Not out of rudeness, but out of not having a head. He was just a big troll body with no head. And the body was now falling forwards toward the Truth Pixie who was still laughing so hard that she couldn't see. So Nikolas quickly dived towards the pixie, hurling her aside, as Sebastian crashed onto the floor, squashing his loose eyeball.

'You saved my life,' said the Truth Pixie, a little bit in love.

'It was nothing.'

Then, the sound of keys in the door.

Nikolas closed his eyes and fought his panic. He was determined now.

'You can do it,' said the Truth Pixie.

'Can I?'

'Of course you can.'

As the door opened Nikolas was back floating up though the air.

'Hey!' shouted an elf guard.

Father Topo's words came back to Nikolas. *You just close your eyes and wish for something to happen.* Perhaps a wish was just a hope with a better aim.

If you wished hard enough maybe all kinds of things could happen. He thought about how Father Vodol had made furniture move. Maybe, with enough determination, a chimney could move too.

'I can do it,' Nikolas said.

'Yes, you can,' agreed the Pixie.

He closed his eyes and wished that he could. Nothing. Stillness. Then warmth, as the wish filled his whole body. He felt a sudden dip in his stomach like he was falling. Or rising.

Then his heart began to race.

When he finally opened his eyes he saw blackness. He was *inside* the chimney.

He could hear his mother's voice. 'My boy! My sweet Christmas boy!'

'I'm going to be like you, Mum! I'm going to make people happy!'

The chimney bent, twisted and expanded to fit him perfectly as he travelled with considerable speed upwards. He could hear the voice of the Truth Pixie somewhere below him, saying, 'Told you!'

And then, in no time at all, Nikolas shot out of the chimney, felt the rush of cool air, before he landed hard but painlessly on the steep tower roof.

Blitzen to the Rescue!

The sun was rising. Raw pinks and oranges filled the sky. It was Christmas Eve. He gazed down at Elfhelm, which seemed as small and harmless as a toy village.

He tried to lift his feet from the tiled roof. But no. Nothing. Maybe he was too scared. He heard an elf guard shout out of a tower window to another elf on the path below.

'Help!' shouted the guard. 'The human boy has escaped!'

'He's on the roof!' said the elf below. It was the one Nikolas had sat opposite at the feast in the village hall. The one with the plaits. Ri-Ri.

Nikolas tried to think. He looked at the elf village below. He saw the reindeer in the field. Then he saw Blitzen, tiny in the distance, nibbling the grass beside the frozen lake.

'Blitzen!' he shouted at the top of his voice, waking up the whole village. 'Blitzen! Over here! It's me, Nikolas!'

He then saw a hundred elf guards in black trousers and tunics running quickly out of the village hall, like insects spreading across the snow. He also saw Father Vodol, shouting orders at them from an upstairs window. Although they were small he knew they could run fast. He didn't have long.

'Blitzen!'

He imagined he could see Blitzen stopping to look up at him.

'Blitzen! Help me! You've got to help! You can fly, Blitzen! You can fly! The magic that saved us makes reindeer fly! You. Can. Fly!'

It was useless. It was in fact a kind of torture to see that mountain, to know the rest of the world was right there beyond. Desperation flooded through him. Even if Blitzen could have understood him, and even if he did have the potential to fly, it is unlikely that he would be able to do so without believing in magic.

Nikolas saw ten or so guards run into the field and climb on to the backs of the reindeer. One by one, the guards urged their mounts into action, kicking their flanks and steering them up towards the tower roof. Within seconds they were galloping fast through the snowy air.

'Blitzen!' he called again, but he could no longer see him. Where was he?

The reindeer and the guards were getting closer to the tower. Shadows in the air. Nikolas sensed a looming dark figure. He could feel him, like a cloud blocking out the sun, getting inside his head, penetrating his mind. Trying to push Nikolas forward, off the roof. And then Father Vodol was actually there, on a reindeer, leading the charge, his beard flecked with snow and his face purple with rage. He was carrying an axe that Nikolas recognised instantly. Long dark handle and dazzling blade.

'Your beloved father left this behind!' shouted Father Vodol, hurling the axe directly at Nikolas who ducked just in time. The axe curved back and landed in Father Vodol's hand, ready for him to try again, as Donner – the reindeer he was riding – circled around the tower roof.

'Get away,' Nikolas said. 'You have no control over me.' He closed his eyes – warmth and light pushed away the dark cloud – and then it was happening. He was in the air, rising. For a second it felt like the snow was falling even faster. He blinked his eyes open, and there was Vodol. In an instant Nikolas had crashed back onto the roof, causing some tiles to come loose and slide off and tumble to the earth below. He slid down too until he was hanging off the edge. He looked down. He could see a crowd of tiny, tiny elves had now gathered on the path to watch the commotion far above.

'Catch the son of Joel the Woodcutter!' shouted one, an elf girl named Snowflake, with shining white hair.

'Kill the son of Joel the Woodcutter!' shouted another, called Picklewick, who was watching the scene through one of his hand-made telescopes and was surprised at his own anger. 'Crush his bones and use them to season your gingerbread! No outsiders!'

'No outsiders!' said Snowflake.

'No outsiders!' said everyone.

'No outsiders! No outsiders! No outsiders!'

Well, actually, not absolutely everyone was shouting this. There was one voice of reason, but it was a very small light voice, yet so clear

as a bell the words managed
to rise up through the air to
Nikolas.

'Leave him alone!' It felt
beautiful to Nikolas's ears, and
gave him hope, and for a
moment his loneliness left
him. It was the voice of
Little Noosh.

'Leave him be!
We're elves!' Father

Topo was now shouting. 'Where has our kindness gone? Come on, we're elves. We didn't used to be like this.'

Nikolas's shoulders burned with pain as he hauled himself back up onto the cold slate roof in time to see the largest reindeer of them all charging towards him, urging himself closer, overtaking the others.

His eyes were fixed on

the roof with the same determination that had helped him climb the mountain.

'Blitzen!'

Father Vodol had seen him too.

'Fire!' he shouted. A guard knelt in the snow and aimed his carefully made longbow – or, as this was an elf – a *shortbow* at them. He pulled the string back with his teeth as he grabbed an arrow, positioned it, and fired. A dark line sped through the air, and whistled past Nikolas's ear. Father Vodol, roaring with frustration, threw the axe at Blitzen and it span through the air, but Blitzen ducked down, fast, and dipped his head so the arrow narrowly missed its target and sliced off the tip of one of his antlers instead. Nikolas ran forward, keeping his eyes on Blitzen and hoping as much as anyone can hope, and leapt into the air. He closed his eyes, hoped some more. The hope was answered. He landed on Blitzen's back.

'Stop them!' screamed Father Vodol.

'Go, go, go!' shouted Nikolas, as Blitzen galloped at incredible speed through the air. 'South! To the mountain!'

And they flew on, dodging flying axes and streaming arrows, until sheer hope and determination led them towards the sunrise.

The Search

They flew through the blustery air over forests full of snow-covered spruce trees and icy lakes. A landscape of white land and silver water. There were no signs of human life. No signs of Christmas Eve excitement. From up high, the land looked as still and flat as a map. They were travelling so fast that what would have taken them a day by land took them only minutes. The cold wind was strong, but Nikolas hardly felt it. Indeed, since he'd been drimwicked he had barely noticed the cold. No, that wasn't quite true. He had been *aware* of the cold, but it hadn't bothered him. It just *was*.

Nikolas felt such relief that he had escaped and at the possibility that his father was alive, such delight and wonder that he could make magic that he suddenly right there, half a mile above a lake, let out the biggest laugh of his life. It was a laugh that came from deep inside his belly. Less of a 'ha ha ha' and more of a 'ho ho ho!'

The kind of jolly laugh his mother used to have.

He leant forward and wrapped his arms around Blitzen.

'You are a true friend!' he told him. 'And I'm sorry about what happened to your antler.'

Blitzen gave a quick raise of his head, as if to say 'that's all right' and galloped on.

They were headed directly south, following the only road, the most obvious route, towards home. Nikolas wondered if his father was already there, perhaps back in the forest chopping wood.

By mid-morning a grey mist had settled around them and doubt began to creep into his head. What if Nikolas's father *had* kidnapped Little Kip? He dismissed the thought. No, his dear papa would never do something like that. That would be impossible. Wouldn't it?

With a heavy heart Nikolas realised what he had to do before he could return home. He had to find Little Kip. He had to find the truth. He had to prove to the elves that his father was a good man. There must be some explanation.

Little Kip had probably just run away from home, just as Nikolas had. All he needed to do was find the elf boy and everything would become clear.

So they flew on and on and on. The reindeer swooped low above forests and higher over fields and the broad clay plains that seemed to stretch towards infinity in the hope they might see Little Kip.

The only thing they didn't do was fly directly over towns because Nikolas didn't know how people might react to seeing a boy on a reindeer flying over their heads. But sometimes they *did* see people. Which made Blitzen happy.

You see, the other thing Nikolas had realised about Blitzen was that he had a sense of humour. And the thing he found really funny was weeing on people. He'd hold it in, for as long as possible, and then when he saw someone far below he'd just, well, *wee*. And the people in question would just think it was raining.

'That's not a very nice Christmas present, Blitzen!' Nikolas said, but he couldn't help laughing.

On and on they travelled, fast and slow and low and high, north and east and south and west, but without success. Nikolas felt increasingly desperate. Maybe he should just go home after all. He was beginning to feel so tired and he knew Blitzen must be even more so. It had started snowing again.

'Come on,' said Nikolas, 'we need to rest for the night.' He had spotted a forest of pine trees immediately to the west. 'Let's land over there and find some shelter.' So Blitzen, ever responsive to Nikolas's commands, angled westwards and flew lower and lower, weaving between the snow-capped pine trees, until they saw a break in the branches, just beyond a ravine.

'This is going to be a strange Christmas,' thought Nikolas.

They settled, amid the tall looming trees, beneath a canopy of branches. Nikolas and Blitzen lay back-to-back, and just as Nikolas was starting to drift into a dreamless sleep he heard something.

A crack of a twig.

Voices.

Men's voices.

Nikolas sat bolt upright and listened hard. It was pitch black now, but the man speaking – in a slow, strong voice – seemed familiar. Nikolas gasped.

It was the voice of the man who had visited his father. Anders the hunter.

'Blitzen,' Nikolas whispered. 'I think it's them. Wait there.' And Nikolas got to his feet and tiptoed carefully over the dry ground.

He saw a gold and orange glow. It grew brighter. A campfire. Shadows were moving like dark ghosts. As he got closer he could see a group of large huddled silhouettes sitting around the fire, talking. The voices were more distinct now.

'We're only days away from Turku,' said one. 'We'll be there by New Year!'

'A week away until we give our little present to the king!' said another.

'I thought we were going home first,' said a voice he knew better than any voice in the world. The sound of it caused Nikolas's heart to miss a beat. Fear and love flooded through him. He was about to shout out 'Papa', but something stopped him and he simply waited, quiet in the stillness of the night.

'No, we promised. The king has to have it before the New Year.'

Nikolas could hardly breathe. His heart was thumping in his chest, but he knew he must try and stay calm. *Be the forest.*

'Well, I promised my son I would be home by now.'

'It depends which promise you want to keep! The one to the king, or the one to your son!'

The sound of laughter filled the forest, echoing off the trees so that it felt like it was coming from everywhere. Birds flapped away from their branches, squawking in fear.

'We better be quiet,' one of the men said, 'or we'll wake him.'

'Oh,' said another, 'don't worry about it. Elves sleep soundly!'

Nikolas's stomach felt too light, as if he was falling. He thought he was going to be sick. Or collapse.

'What does it matter?' said Anders. 'He's in a cage. It's not as if he can go anywhere.'

It was true!

Nikolas strained his eyes to see beyond the trees. There, on the other side of the fire and the men, was a strange box-shaped thing. He couldn't quite see the elf boy, but he knew that he was there. The men carried on talking.

'Just keep thinking of the money, Joel. You'll never have to worry about Christmas again.'

'All that money.'

'What would you do with it? What would you buy for Christmas?'

'I'd buy a farm.'

'I'd just look at it,' said another one, who was called Aatu, though Nikolas didn't know that yet. Aatu had a very large head with a very small brain inside. He had wild hair and a wild beard which made him look like someone peeping through a bush. 'And after I looked at it I'd buy a toilet.'

'A toilet? What's a toilet?'

'It's a new invention. I heard about it. The king's got one. It's a magic chamber pot. With bowels like mine it's got to be a good investment. And I'd buy a really nice candle. I like candles. I'd buy a big red candle.'

The men fell to murmuring among themselves and Nikolas took his chance. Crouching on his hands and knees he crept slowly forwards, dodging pine cones, breathing slowly as he weaved through the trees, always keeping a safe distance from the men.

Eventually, he reached the cage. It was made of wood and tied firmly with rope to the solid timber of a sleigh. A painted sleigh. The sleigh engraved with the word 'Christmas'. His sleigh. Inside the cage, curled up, was a little elf boy.

He wore the same kind of deep green tunic – and looked roughly the same age – as Little Noosh. He had brown, very straight hair and large ears, even for an elf, but a tiny nose. And though his far-apart eyes were closed, he had a down-turned mouth and his face was creased with worry.

Nikolas remembered his own brief but horrible time as a prisoner. He stood there wondering what he could do. There was no path. Just trees to one side, and the clearing to the other. He was trembling with fear but he knew he must wait for his father and the other men to fall asleep.

Little Kip opened his eyes and stared straight at Nikolas. For a moment it looked as if he was going to scream.

'Sssh,' Nikolas said softly, with his finger on his lips. 'I'm here to help you.'

Little Kip was still a very young elf, and although he didn't know Nikolas he was skilled at spotting goodness inside someone, and could see the kindness in Nikolas's eyes. He seemed to understand.

'I'm scared,' said the elf, in elf.

But Nikolas understood. 'It's all right.'

'Is it?'

'Well, no. Not right now. But it will be . . .'

But then, a fierce rough voice seemed to come out of nowhere. 'Happy Christmas.'

Nikolas turned around and saw one of the men, a tall skinny man with a crooked face wearing a woollen hat with flaps over his ears. He was pointing an arrow and crossbow at him.

'Who are you? Tell me. Or you're dead.'

The Elf Boy

'm just lost in the forest,' Nikolas stammered. 'I'm not causing any trouble.'

'Hey!' shouted the man. 'I asked you who you are. It's the middle of the night. You're up to something. Tell me or I'll put an arrow through you.'

Nikolas heard some of the other men, waking up, talking, confused.

'I'm Nikolas. I'm just . . . a boy.'

'A boy wandering the forest in the middle of the night!'

'Oh no, oh no, oh no,' said Little Kip. Or maybe it was 'Oh no, oh no, oh no, oh no'. But anyway, to all human ears except Nikolas, it just sounded like 'keebum, keebum, keebum.'

Then some footsteps, and a familiar voice. 'I know who he is,' said Anders, as he loomed over Nikolas. 'He's Joel's son. Put the crossbow down, Toivo. He isn't here for trouble. That's right, isn't it, boy?'

More shadows. The other men – five of them – were walking towards him.

His father spoke up. 'Nikolas? Is that you?' he asked. Total disbelief.

Nikolas looked into his father's face and felt scared. Maybe it was because he had grown a beard. Or maybe it was something else. The eyes, those familiar eyes, now seemed dark and distant, like those of a stranger. Nikolas was so overwhelmed he could hardly speak.

'Papa. Yes, it's me.'

Joel ran over and threw his arms around his son. He hugged Nikolas till he thought his ribs would break. Nikolas hugged him back, trying to believe he was still the good father he had always imagined him to be. He felt his father's beard prickle his cheek. It felt lovely, comforting.

'What are you doing here?' Nikolas sensed quiet urgency in his father's question.

He didn't know what to say, but he decided to do what his mother had taught him to do when he was in trouble. He took a deep breath and told the truth. 'I wasn't getting on with Aunt Carlotta. So I went to look for you. And so I headed to the Far North, and found Elfhelm . . . And then the elves put me in prison.'

His father's face softened, his eyes crinkled, and he seemed familiar again. 'Oh, Nikolas, my poor boy! What happened?'

'They locked me in the tower because they don't trust humans.'

Nikolas looked at the elf shackled to the cage by his wrists and ankles and then behind him at the six other men who were standing in the moonlight. Nikolas desperately wanted him to tell them to go away. He wanted to believe in his father and continued to hope that this was all a mix-up, a misunderstanding.

'Well, son,' his father said, drawing himself up to his full height and looking very solemn. 'I have to say, those stories I told you about how happy and kind the elves were, were just that – stories. I discovered that the elves aren't who we thought they would be.'

Nikolas looked at Little Kip who was staring at him, beseechingly, from his cage. The elf was too scared to speak. And Nikolas couldn't help but feel betrayed, as if everything he had ever known was a lie. 'You didn't tell me you were going to kidnap an elf. You said you were going to find proof of Elfhelm.'

'Yes,' said his father, seemingly eager and sincere. 'And what could be better proof than a real-life elf?'

'But you *lied* to me.'

'I didn't lie. I didn't quite know what kind of proof we would find. I just didn't tell you the whole truth.'

Nikolas looked at the large menacing gang of men in the dark and silent forest. 'Did they make you do it, Papa?'

Anders laughed and the others followed, sending a clatter of voices through the forest.

Joel winced. 'No. No one made me do it.'

'Tell him, Joel,' said Anders. 'Why don't you tell him what really happened?'

Joel nodded, nervously looking at his son. He swallowed. 'Well, Nikolas, in fact, it was my idea. When Anders came to me that night, I suggested it. I said the best evidence would be if we got a real-life elf and took it to the king.'

Nikolas couldn't believe what he was hearing. The words stung him like vinegar in a cut. His own father was a kidnapper. Most people grow up gradually, over many years, but standing there in the still forest, Nikolas lost his childhood in a second. Nothing makes you grow up quicker than discovering your father is not the man you think he is.

'How could you do that?'

His father sighed. It was a long sigh. 'It's a

lot of money, Nikolas. Three thousand rubles. That could buy us a cow. Or . . . or a pig. We'll be able to have a very good Christmas next year. The kind of Christmas me and Carlotta never knew. I'll be able to buy you toys.'

'Or a toilet!' said Aartu, from somewhere behind his beard.

Joel ignored his dim-witted friend and carried on. 'I'll be able to buy a horse and a new cart. We'd ride into town, and people would look at us, admire us, and be jealous of how much money we have.'

Anger bubbled inside Nikolas. 'Why? I don't want people to be jealous! I want people to be happy!'

Joel looked back to the other men, who were clearly entertained by this conversation. He frowned with frustration and turned back to Nikolas. 'Well, you need to learn about the world, my son. You're a child, and I'm not, and I know about the world. It's a selfish place. No one will look after you. You have to look after yourself. And that's what I'm doing, all right? No one was ever kind to me. No one ever gave me presents. I used to cry, every Christmas Day, because I never got a single thing. Other children had at least one little present from their parents. But me and Carlotta, we had nothing. But next birthday, next Christmas, I can buy you anything you want . . .'

Nikolas looked again at the cage, and the ropes. 'I was happy with the sleigh. I was happy with you and Miika. I was even happy with the turnip-doll!'

'Next Christmas you'll thank me. Not this one. It's too late for that. But next one. You'll see. I promise.'

'*No,*' said Nikolas. Just saying the word felt like turning a key inside his mind, locking out any weakness.

'What are you talking about?'

Nikolas took a big breath, as if inhaling courage. 'No. I'm going to take Little Kip back to Elfhelm. Back to his home.'

The men laughed some more. The sound clattered through Nikolas, making him feel scared and angry at the same time. One of them − a gruff-voiced man with a coat made of reindeer skin − snarled, 'No, you're not. Tell him, Toivo.'

Toivo raised his crossbow again, and spat on the ground.

Joel turned to see the weapon. 'I'm sorry, Nikolas, but you're not taking him back. There's too much at stake.'

'If you loved me more than you loved money, then you would do it. Papa, please. Toys are great. But being good is better than being rich. You could never be happy as a kidnapper.'

'I've never been happy as a woodcutter, either,' said Joel, his face screwed up as if he was in pain. 'Now, if all goes according to plan I'll have a chance to find out what life has to offer.'

Nikolas shook his head. He began to cry. He couldn't help it. There was too much inside him. Anger, fear, disappointment. He loved his father, and yet this man who he loved had stolen an elf boy from his own home and put him in a cage.

Nikolas wiped his eyes with the back of his hand. He thought of Father Topo's words to Little Noosh. *We must never let fear be our guide.* 'Let's take the elf back,' said Nikolas, in a louder voice, looking around at all of the men. 'The elves would be happy. They might even give us a reward. We must take Little Kip back to his family.'

'They'd kill us!' said Anders with confidence. Anders had his bow and grey-feathered arrows slung on his back. 'Listen, boy, why don't you come with us? It could be an adventure. You'll get to meet the king.'

'No way, he'll ruin everything,' said the gruff-voiced man with the reindeer coat.

'Silence, Tomas,' said Anders. 'This is Joel's son . . . Come on, boy, what do you say?'

For a brief moment Nikolas thought how it would be to go to the royal palace and meet King Frederick. He pictured his face from the back of a coin, and the cuddly toy he had always seen in the toyshop window. With his large nose and big chin and splendid crown and clothes. Everything would be made of gold. Maybe his whole palace was made

of gold. It would have been wonderful to go there. But nothing was as wonderful as doing the right thing.

'Come with us, son,' said Joel softly now. 'Don't be silly. Anders is right. It will be an adventure. A Christmas adventure. Anders could teach you how to shoot a bow and arrow – wouldn't that be fun?'

'Yes,' said Anders. 'You could help me shoot a deer. And then you could cook it on a fire. We've been eating fresh meat every night. You look as though you could do with a good meal, and there's no better meal than one you shoot yourself. One day, I even shot a reindeer, but it got away before I had time to kill it. Disappeared into the woods.'

Nikolas thought of the grey-feathered arrow sticking out of Blitzen's leg. He knew that, before long, Blitzen would be coming to look for him. And then these big, tall men would probably try and kill him again, and turn him into a reindeer stew. He looked into Little Kip's large strange eyes which were filled with fear. Little Kip still hadn't said a word, and in that moment, for the first time in his life, Nikolas hated his father.

He turned to all the other men, standing there in the frosty forest, solid shadows in the blue-black of the night. Kidnappers. Reindeer killers. He was scared but he was also determined.

'It's all right, Little Kip, I'm going to get you out of here and take you home.'

Blitzen's Revenge

ontrol your boy!' one of the men shouted. Nikolas ignored him. He was concentrating hard on the metal chains that kept Little Kip shackled to the cage on the sleigh.

He felt his father's hand grab his arm and try to pull him away. 'Come on, Nikolas, you're embarrassing us both now.'

'Put him in the cage too!' suggested Toivo.

'We can't put a boy in a cage,' said Anders.

'You already have,' said Nikolas. 'Or don't elves count?'

'No, son,' said Joel. 'Of course they don't count. They're elves! The elves were quite happy to put you in prison. Remember?'

Nikolas thought about Father Vodol, remembered the fury in his voice and how frightened he had felt.

'Yes, but . . .' But *what*? For a moment, Nikolas wondered what he was doing. Why did he care? Then he looked inside the cage.

Little Kip was fretting, his face twitching all over.

'You're an elf!' whispered Nikolas, urgently. 'You've got magic in you! Use your powers.'

Little Kip began to cry again. 'I can't! It's impossible!'

'You can't say that word! You're too young to swear!'

Little Kip looked at him, tilting his head to one side.

Nikolas knew that he was asking a lot of a young elf. Little Kip was, well, *little*. It was hard to work out elf ages but he couldn't have been much more than five years old. Maybe his magic hadn't developed yet. And even if it had, then Nikolas knew it wasn't that easy without the confidence of a single, clear wish. Magic was useless by itself. Making impossibilities possibilities was harder than it looked.

The elf closed his eyes, straining. The men started to jeer.

'It's Christmas Eve,' urged Nikolas. 'Can you feel it? There's magic in the air. Come on, Little Kip. Use your drimwick powers. You can do it.'

'No,' came a tiny voice. 'I can't.'

'You can. I know you can. You're an elf. You can do it.'

Little Kip frowned hard.

'Come away, Nikolas. I mean it,' said Joel, grabbing Nikolas's hand.

There was a strange tinkling sound. The little elf was changing colour with the effort, his face becoming as purple as a plum. Then: *clank*.

Nikolas saw one of the iron chains between the elf's handcuffs snap like toffee.

Then another.

And another.

There was only one more.

'That's it, Little Kip. You're doing it.'

'Look, he's escaping!'

'Stop your sorcery, you pointy-eared little freak!' Toivo spat at the elf. 'Or I'll shoot you dead.' Toivo raised his crossbow and pointed it at Little Kip.

'I will not,' said the elf. Which to the men, sounded like 'Kalabash animbo.'

'And stop your gobbledegook,' added Toivo.

Somewhere above, a bird flapped away from a tree.

'A dead elf's no good to us,' said Joel.

'A dead elf is better than an escaped elf.'

Toivo spat again. 'If it makes another move, I'll shoot it.'

Nikolas pulled his hand away, fast, from his father's grip. He had never felt less like his father's son. He darted to the front of the cage. He could hardly control his breathing. The fear was intense. He looked up at Toivo and his dark desperate eyes, which seemed to contain the night. 'Well, I'm not going to let you.'

'Don't tempt me, little boy. I could kill you too.' His voice didn't falter.

Tomas gasped. 'Look!'

Nikolas turned and saw a whirl of snow and hooves and hot breath. The forest was rumbling as though filled with thunder. It was a huge reindeer, pounding towards them.

'Blitzen!' called Nikolas, fearing for the creature's life.

'Leave him to me!' shouted Anders.

He fired an arrow, and it whistled through the air, fast and straight. Blitzen kept galloping, even faster, seemingly towards the arrow, but at the last minute he lifted his head up and his whole body with it, and left the ground at a steep angle. Climbing through the air as if on an invisible hill, brushing past snow-covered pine branches as he rose.

Nikolas watched Anders's bow and arrow aim higher as the reindeer pawed the sky, antlers silhouetted against the moon.

'Don't shoot him! Please! He's my only friend!' pleaded Nikolas.

Joel looked at his son's white, thin face. Then he looked at his own left hand. At his half-finger. 'Life is pain,' he said, sadly.

'But it's also magic, Papa.'

Joel ignored him. 'You need to calm him down, Nikolas. He'll be safer if you call him back down, where we can see him. We won't shoot him, will we, men? We'll capture him and take him to the king. Sure he'd like to see a flying reindeer.'

Anders lowered his arrow. 'Yes. Call him down.'

'Blitzen!' called Nikolas, wondering if any of them could truly be trusted. 'Come down from the sky! It's safer.'

And the reindeer seemed to understand because a minute later he had landed in the little clearing, chest heaving and eyes shining with exertion.

'This is Blitzen. Please don't hurt him,' said Nikolas. The reindeer nuzzled his neck.

'Lake Blitzen,' said Tomas, smoothing down his reindeer-skin coat.

Nikolas stroked the creature's neck, and Blitzen stared at Anders, making a noise between a grunt and a growl.

'It's all right, Blitzen. He's not going to hurt you again,' said Nikolas, wishing he could truly believe what he was saying.

But even as he was saying it, Toivo was raising his crossbow.

'No, Toivo!' cried Joel. Nikolas tried to think, looking around him, as if the answer could be found somewhere in the scary darkness of the forest.

There was only one thing to do. 'Okay. We'll come with you on the adventure. I would love to meet the king.'

'He's lying,' said Toivo.

Joel looked into his son's eyes, and in that instant Nikolas knew that he understood, as perhaps only a father can. 'No. He's not. You aren't, are you, Nikolas? Because if you *are* lying you will be killed and there will be nothing I can do about it.'

'No, Papa.' Nikolas took a deep breath. 'I'm not lying. I've changed my mind. I was being stupid. The elves locked me in prison with a murderous troll. I don't owe them anything.'

There were a few moments when no one

spoke. The only sound was the cold wind whispering through the trees.

Then Anders thumped Nikolas on the shoulder. 'Good boy. You've done the right thing. Hasn't he, Joel?'

'Yes,' said Joel. 'He always does.'

'Well, good. That's settled. We better get some rest now,' said Anders. 'Big day tomorrow.' He put his arms around Tomas and Toivo.

'The boy and the reindeer must sleep away from the elf creature. Just to be safe,' said Tomas.

'I'm fine with that,' said Nikolas.

Joel wasn't entirely happy. 'But wait, what about the elf? What if he uses his magic? One of us needs to stay on guard, to make sure he doesn't escape.'

'Good point,' said Toivo, rubbing his eyes. 'I'll do it.'

'Toivo, you're too tired,' said Anders. 'You've drunk too much cloudberry wine as always. We need someone else.'

'I feel wide awake,' said Joel. 'I'll do it. It's my son who's been causing trouble. I feel I'm to blame.'

'All right, then. That makes sense. Wake me at first light and I'll take over.'

Anders pointed to the pines on the other

side of the campfire, beyond the clearing, towards the ravine. 'You can sleep over there.' He patted Blitzen on the back, smoothed his snow-damp fur.

'Sorry, old buddy. No hard feelings about the arrow, eh?'

Blitzen thought about this and, as he did so took a wee on Anders's long johns.

'Hey!' cried Anders, and Tomas burst into laughter. Anders couldn't help laughing too, which caused the other men to join in.

And so it was that the men all went back to sleep by the still-glowing campfire, and Nikolas and Blitzen lay down amid the trees beyond them, and Joel stayed sitting in front of the cage containing Little Kip. Whether Little Kip had given up on his chances of escape it was hard to tell, but Nikolas certainly hadn't stopped dreaming of helping him. He lay snuggled into Blitzen, their bodies warming each other as the voices of the men became silent.

'Happy Christmas, Blitzen,' he said, glumly, but the reindeer was already asleep.

Something Good

Nikolas lay awake, staring up at the full moon for a long time. As he was drifting off to sleep he heard a noise. No more than a whisper, lost in the wind. He looked up, and saw his father, slowly pushing the sleigh towards him and away from the camp. The elf couldn't have been very heavy because the sleigh was moving easily. Little Kip was inside the cage, silent and wide-eyed, holding onto the bars.

'What are you doing?' whispered Nikolas.

Joel put a finger to his lips, then took the rope harness he'd been using to pull the sleigh off his shoulders and went over to Blitzen to put it over his head.

Nikolas couldn't believe it.

'I knew you were going to try and free the elf,' said Joel. 'Which is really a terrible idea, by the way. Really, really terrible. But it is Christmas. And your birthday. And you're still my son. And I want you to stay alive. So help me.'

Nikolas leant in towards Blitzen. 'Stay calm,' he said, in a voice so quiet the reindeer might not even have heard him. Blitzen slowly got up and stood stock still as they put the harness over him. The fire had died now and the men were still sleeping their drunken sleep. Nikolas felt nervous, but also strangely happy and relieved. His father still had goodness in him after all.

One of the men – maybe Toivo, though it was too dark and distant to tell – rolled over and grumbled a little. Nikolas and Joel held their breath and waited for him to settle.

The harness was on.

'Okay, we're ready,' whispered Joel, as the wind dropped. It was as if the forest was straining to listen to their plans. 'Now get on your reindeer and fly away.'

'Papa, please come with us.'

'No. I'll slow you down.'

'Blitzen's strong. And fast. You could be on

the sleigh, making sure that Little Kip is okay. You can't stay here. They'll kill you.'

Toivo – yes, it was definitely Toivo – his long skinny frame moving as he lay in the dark, was clearly visible now.

Nikolas had never seen his father this frightened before. Even when faced with the bear. And the fear he saw in his father's face quickened Nikolas's heart.

'All right,' said Joel. 'I'll get on the sleigh. We've got to go. Quick.'

Nikolas climbed on Blitzen's back. Then he leant forward to whisper in the reindeer's ear. 'Come on, boy, as fast as you can. Let's get out of here.'

Now Toivo was properly awake. He was kicking at the boots of the other men and urging them to wake up.

'They're escaping!'

Blitzen heaved towards a clear line between the trees, struggling as he switched from walk to trot.

'Come on, Blitzen. You can do it, boy. Come on! It's Christmas Day! Use your magic!'

Nikolas heard a strange hushed whistle. To his horror he saw an arrow speeding through the air. He ducked, saving his head by a fraction.

Blitzen was having difficulty breaking into a gallop – with the weight of the sleigh and the cage and Little Kip and Joel and Nikolas. A second arrow whooshed by.

Blitzen gained speed, but not enough. The trees were too close together. He weaved dangerously through them. Nikolas, holding on for dear life, turned to see the sledge tilt to the left, nearly tipping Joel off.

Nikolas could hardly think, his brain a chaos of trees and speed and fear.

Arrows and stones were now flying though the air.

And then, the very worst thing of all happened.

Nikolas heard a scream behind him – an agonised howl which tore through the night. He turned to see his father, who was standing at the very edge of the sleigh, with a piece of thin, feathered wood jutting out from his shoulder. Blood was already leaking out onto his patchwork shirt.

'Papa!' Nikolas cried as another arrow whistled by his ear.

Then Nikolas felt Blitzen's weight, pressing upwards. It was happening.

But as they started to leave the ground, a rock

from the catapult hit Blitzen's chest. Perhaps it was the shock or the pain but he weakened momentarily. He tried to tilt back and lift higher as they went over the men's heads. But Nikolas could see they were in trouble, they were going *into* the trees and not *over* them. His face was whipped by the snowy branches, and he choked on pine needles, as arrows continued to fly by, streaking black lines in the dark.

'Come on, Blitzen!' cried Nikolas, urging the reindeer on to defy gravity. But poor Blitzen was struggling. He crashed back to earth but kept galloping, trying to lift off again.

'It's too . . . heavy,' moaned Joel, in agony as his hand clutched his shoulder.

Nikolas knew his father was right but he noticed that the trees up ahead were thinning.

'It'll be all right!' shouted Nikolas. 'Come on, Blitzen!'

Nikolas felt Blitzen's feet tread on nothing but air, a soft floating upward, but still it was no good. His whole body was tight with effort and the sleigh was dragging them back down. Nikolas tried to use his own magic. Fear had turned his mind into a cyclone of thoughts, so he couldn't hold a wish for long before it flew away like paper in the wind.

'You don't understand!' shouted Joel. 'The ravine! The river!'

And then Nikolas understood. It wasn't just the trees that stopped ahead of them. It was the land too. It disappeared into nothing, like a horizon that was too close, too low. They were only metres away from a deep, deep dark drop towards the river.

'You won't be able to cross! The only way is to fly!' shouted Joel. 'It's too heavy.'

But Nikolas wasn't giving in. With every nerve in his body, with every molecule inside him, he hoped and prayed and urged the magic – his own and Blitzen's – to work. 'Come on, Blitzen! Come on, boy, you can do it! Fly!'

The reindeer rose again into the air, but only slightly. They crashed into more branches. Joel was holding tightly onto the cage now. Nikolas heard Little Kip whimper in fear.

'Oh no!' said the elf. 'Oh no, oh no, oh no, oh no!'

'I'm weighing you down!' said Joel. 'I'm going to jump.'

The words ripped at Nikolas like teeth.

'No, no, Papa! Don't!'

He turned around. Joel's face was full of another kind of pain now. The pain of farewell.

'*No!*'

'I love you, Nikolas!' he yelled. 'I want you to remember me for something good.'

'No, Papa! It will be . . .'

They were right at the edge now. Nikolas felt it, before he saw it. The sudden lightening, the quickening of Blitzen's pace as Joel let go of the cage and fell to the ground below. Nikolas – tears bursting from his eyes – saw his father curled up in the snow, getting smaller and smaller and finally disappearing

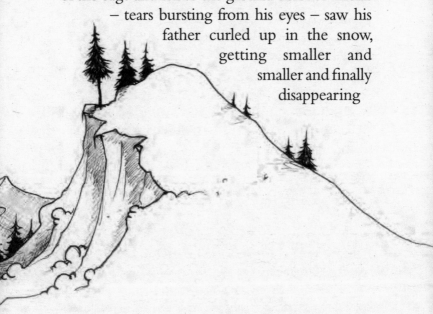

in the darkness. Just as his mother had disappeared into the darkness of the well. Nikolas felt terrified as it dawned on him. He was all alone in the world now.

Blitzen, with a lighter load, and determined to take his cargo to safety, soared high above the ravine, fast and strong, away, into the sky.

Riding Through the Air

The sadness Nikolas felt then was incredible. To lose someone you love is the very worst thing in the world. It creates an invisible hole that you feel you are falling down and will never end. People you love make the world real and solid and when they suddenly go away forever, nothing feels solid any more. He would never hear his father's voice again. Never hold his strong hands. Never see him wear his red hat.

The tears on Nikolas's face froze as he flew through the cold air. It was the saddest birthday, the saddest Christmas ever. He clung to Blitzen's back, feeling his warmth, only occasionally looking behind him to make sure the sleigh and the cage were still there.

With his ear to the reindeer's fur, he could hear the blood pumping around Blitzen's body. It seemed to replace the sound of galloping.

He'd been crying since his father jumped

off the sleigh. Had he died as he had fallen? Or had Anders and Toivo and all the others reached him first? Either way, he feared the result was the same. He would never see his father again. He felt it, a howling emptiness, inside his heart.

Slowly the sky became light.

'I'm sorry,' said a small voice behind him. 'It's all my fault.'

Nikolas had hardly heard Little Kip say a word (except 'oh no') until now.

'Don't be sorry!' Nikolas shouted back, wiping a tear from his eye. 'None of this is your fault!'

A little time went by.

'Thank you for saving me,' came that same small voice.

'Listen, I know you think my father was a bad human. And it was a bad thing he did. But there was good too. He was just weak. We had no money . . . Humans are complicated.'

'Elves too,' said Little Kip.

Nikolas stared into the whiteness of the snow

clouds all around him. Even climbing through small chimneys or flying through the air was easier than believing in life. Yet, as Blitzen galloped on, Nikolas knew that he had to carry on and return Little Kip to his home. He just had to.

'You are a friend,' said Little Kip.

They flew over the mountain, and this time Nikolas could see Elfhelm straight away – the Street of Seven Curves, the tower, the village hall, the Wooded Hills, and the lake.

By the time Blitzen landed right in the centre of the Reindeer Field, a crowd had already gathered. Nikolas wasn't scared because nothing in the world could scare him now. He had lost his father. What terror could the world

offer that was worse than that? Even when, after climbing off the reindeer, he saw the crowd part to make way for Father Vodol, who was marching towards them, he still didn't feel fear. Just emptiness.

'So, the son of Joel the Woodcutter has returned,' said Father Vodol.

Nikolas nodded towards the wooden cage.

'What is going on?'

'I've brought Little Kip back to Elfhelm,' announced Nikolas, loud enough for everyone to hear.

'It's true, Father Vodol,' said a smiling, white-whiskered elf walking towards them. It was Father Topo, closely followed by Little Noosh. 'Nikolas has saved Little Kip! It's the news we've all been waiting for.'

'Yes,' said Father Vodol, offering Nikolas a reluctant smile. 'Yes, I suppose it is. But now the human must go back to the tower.'

The crowd roared in disagreement.

'But it's Christmas Day!'

'Let him be!'

Father Topo shook his head. 'No. Not this time.'

'Enough of this goodwill! Father Topo, no more words out of you. The human must return to the tower. That is it. Final.'

The crowd of elves grew angrier, and a couple of them threw some extra-hard pieces of gingerbread at Father Vodol's head.

Father Topo looked stern for the first time in his life. 'You will have an uprising on your hands. The human boy is a hero.'

And the elves started chanting: 'Hero! Hero! Hero!'

'You ungrateful elves!' shouted Father Vodol at the top of his voice, which was very, very loud. 'Don't you realise all I've done for you? How safe I've helped you become, by ending goodwill and joy?'

'I quite liked goodwill, come to think of it,' said one elf.

'And joy wasn't so bad either,' said another.

'And I miss spickle dancing.'

'Me too!'

'And proper pay! Three chocolate coins isn't enough to live on.'

'And being nice to non-elves.'

And on and on it went, the list of complaints, and Father Vodol, as the democratically elected leader of Elfhelm, realised he had no choice. 'All right,' he said. 'Before we decide what to do with the human boy let us first take Little Kip home.'

And an almighty roar rose up through the crowd and many began spickle dancing, illegally. Nikolas looked around and cried again, but this time his tears had a little bit of happiness in them. The kind of happiness that can only be felt by being around the joy and goodwill of elves.

A Boy Called Christmas

ittle Kip's parents were called Moodon and Loka. They were just humble workers, but with specialisms, so were wearing the blue tunics. Moodon was a gingerbread baker and Loka was a toymaker, specialising in spinning tops, who had fallen on hard times recently, as elves had lost interest in playing. They lived in a cabin on the edge of the village, made of wood, but with gingerbread chairs and tables and cupboards, not far from the Wooded Hills.

Anyway, that's not important. What is important is that Nikolas had never seen anyone look as happy as Moodon and Loka when he brought Little Kip to their doorstep.

'Amazing! It's a miracle!' said Loka, bursting into tears. 'Thank you so much. This is the best Christmas present ever!'

'It is Nikolas you should be thanking,' said Father Topo, pushing the boy forward.

'Oh thank you, thank you, thank you,

Nikolas.' Loka hugged Nikolas's knees tightly, nearly causing him to fall over. 'How can I ever repay you? I will give you some toys! I have lots that I have been making – spinning tops, especially. Wait there.'

'And I'll bake you the *best* gingerbread!' said Moodon, who had ginger hair and a ginger beard. He almost looked like he was made of gingerbread.

Father Vodol couldn't help but frown at the sight of a human being thanked. 'Well, he is an escaped convict, so he should really be going back to the tower.'

Huge tears began to cloud Little Kip's sky-blue eyes.

Nikolas remembered the cold dark tiny furnace room he had been locked inside, and realised – right then – that however bleak life might be without his father, it would be even bleaker spent locked up in a tower.

'As you have seen, that would be a very unpopular decision,' said Father Topo firmly.

'I know it's not my place as I am not on the council but I think this particular human is a hero for rescuing my son. A real Christmas hero!' said Loka.

And even Mother Ri-Ri agreed that Nikolas

shouldn't go back to the tower. 'I think we need to rewrite some of the elf laws,' she suggested.

Father Vodol was not happy. He grumbled. He paced around. A nearby clog detached itself from the clog rack and fell off and clunked on to the floor. Everyone stared at the clog. They knew that it was because Father Vodol was in a bad mood.

'Father Vodol!' said Mother Ri-Ri, appalled.

'I'm sorry. But he is a *human*. We know what humans can do. We can't soften our position on humans because of one child.'

Father Topo clicked his tongue thoughtfully. 'You do realise, this human will help you sell lots of newspapers . . .'

Father Vodol paused. Nikolas could see he was struggling because he knew this to be true. Eventually, in the quietest voice imaginable, a word crept out of the side of Father Vodol's mouth. 'Maybe.'

Father Topo placed a hand on Nikolas's shoulder. Or tried to. It was too much of a stretch, so he patted his arm instead. 'So he can get a pardon?'

There was a very long pause. It was a pause far longer than these two sentences, but eventually the pause came to an end.

Father Vodol nodded the smallest nod that has ever been nodded by elf or human. 'Yes.'

'Hooray!' said everyone who wasn't Father Vodol.

'I think we should throw a Christmas party to celebrate,' said Mother Ri-Ri.

Father Vodol tutted. 'We *had* a Christmas party two days ago.'

'That was a *terrible* party,' spluttered Mother Ri-Ri. 'Come on. He deserves one!'

'I would be very honoured,' said Nikolas. 'But I think tonight me and Blitzen would just like to rest.'

Loka arrived back in the room holding seven spinning tops, a snow globe, a cuddly bear and an art set. The spinning tops in particular looked beautiful. All of them were brightly coloured – reds and greens, mainly, all hand-painted. They were the loveliest toys Nikolas had ever seen. It was too much to carry. Two of the tops fell and spun on the floor.

Father Topo took a biscuit from his pocket and nibbled it thoughtfully. 'Isn't it wonderful? Just the simple act of giving presents.'

'Not really,' said Father Vodol.

'Honestly,' said Nikolas, as Loka tried to pick

up the toys from the floor, 'just one spinning top will be fine!'

Loka shook her head, causing her long plaits to sway from side to side, as even more spinning tops dropped to the floor. 'No. You need more than one spinning top. Spinning tops are very important. They relax you. They take your mind off things. I just need to find something to put all your presents in.' She looked around. Little Kip pointed at his father's stockings.

'Good idea!' agreed Loka. 'Moodon, take off your stockings.'

'What?'

'They're the perfect size for all these spinning tops. Go on. Take them off. You've plenty of others.'

So Moodon took off his woollen stockings, in front of everyone. Nikolas was surprised that elf legs were quite hairy. Well, Moodon's were.

Once they were off, Loka placed all the toys inside. 'See! The perfect size. Perhaps we should always use stockings to carry toys. There you go! Merry Christmas!'

And though stockings full of toys didn't make everything better, Nikolas felt a little happier knowing he had made someone else happier. And then he said goodbye to Little Kip and headed out with Father Topo into the cool night, where Blitzen waited outside, staring at him with loving eyes that sparkled like the snow.

The Big Decision

Blitzen settled back in the Reindeer Field with Donner and Dasher and Vixen and all the others, and over the next few weeks Nikolas observed that the reindeer seemed to like Blitzen's naughty sense of humour.

They were always laughing at him. Well, it was impossible to tell if the reindeer were really laughing, as reindeer laughter is very hard to detect, but their eyes shone brighter whenever he was around.

And Nikolas stayed in Father Topo's cabin. He stayed there for many weeks. He ate the delicious gingerbread that Moodon made and enjoyed playing cards (each one hand-painted by Loka) with Little Noosh. Little Noosh, like all elves, was amazing at card games but occasionally she would let him win. He mixed well, and made friends with elves, and was never snobby, regardless of the colour of their tunic.

The sadness inside him was strong, though. He tried to remember the good side of his father. It had always been there, underneath, like the bright red beneath the dirt on his hat. Nikolas washed the hat and wore it and he was determined for that good side to live on inside himself, and for him never to lose it.

'I've been thinking,' said Nikolas, after a month in Elfhelm. 'It's time for me to go back to the human world.'

'Well,' Father Topo would say, 'if that is what you want to do, then you should do it.'

And one day he even got Blitzen to fly him to Kristiinankaupunki. As he flew, he occasionally looked for his father, the way he had looked for him before. But of course there was now no father to be found. They landed on the church roof, and Nikolas climbed down the tower. He spent the day among the humans. He stared in the window of the toyshop, at the elf dolls that looked far too square and simple to be elves. He saw the cuddly doll of King Frederick. He saw a boy walking out with the wooden reindeer. He remembered that craving inside him, when he used to gaze in with his dad, to have the toys that other children had. Now all he did was crave to be by his father's side.

The plan had been to go back to the cottage,

but there was no way. Why choose to live with a nasty aunt when you could live in a place of joy and magic? Why live in a place so full of reminders of a past that can't be brought back? So he made the decision. He was going to live with the elves for ever.

But as Nikolas kept banging his head on the roof beams at Father Topo's cabin, it was decided that he should have a home of his own. So the elves built him a pinewood house, with some gingerbread and candy cane furniture. The only thing Nikolas had been certain to ask the architects for was a view of the Reindeer Field. So they built the house right on the edge of the snow-covered grass, meaning that from all the south-facing windows he could see Blitzen at any time.

Sometimes, when Blitzen was in a good mood, he would fly circuits around Nikolas's house, galloping fast through the air past all the upstairs windows. Occasionally, some of the other reindeer joined in – Prancer and Comet, usually, and sometimes Dasher, though never Donner, as she was far too sensible. Nikolas felt lucky. He thought of Aunt Carlotta and sleeping out in the cold. There were many worse ways to live as an eleven-year-old boy, than surrounded by magic and elves and reindeer.

When he was twelve, Nikolas was elected to the Elf Council after being nominated for election by Father Topo. Even Father Vodol supported this idea, as he knew that it would make another good front page for the *Daily Snow*. Particularly because Nikolas was the youngest person, or elf, ever to be honoured in this way.

Then, as Father Vodol had stepped down as elf leader, to return to his media work, there was another election. For the leadership of Elfhelm.

Nikolas won the election by seven thousand, nine hundred and eighty-three votes, with only one elf voting against the idea.

So Nikolas was called Father Nikolas, which struck Nikolas as funny, as he was only twelve and clearly not a father, but that was the custom in Elfhelm. Mother Vodol, Father Vodol's much cheerier younger sister, suggested that he should have an elf name, as Nikolas sounded a bit too like neekalis, a very disgusting troll cheese.

'Yes,' agreed Mother Ri-Ri. 'I don't want to be reminded of mouldy cheese every time I say your name!'

'Oh y-y-yes,' said Mother Breer, the nervous beltmaker who had recently been appointed as a council member, following a sympathy vote in her favour after she had been burgled by a gang of pixies. 'That is t-t-t-t-true. "Neekalis" is a very bad word. It is n-n-nearly as bad as "stinky m-m-m-m-mudfungle". Or "impossible". We must think of s-s-something else.'

At which point Father Topo interrupted: 'How about we ask Nikolas?'

There was only one name that came to mind.

'Christmas,' said Nikolas.

'What about Christmas?' grumbled Father Vodol. 'It is seven months away.'

'No, I mean, why don't you call me Christmas? Father Christmas.'

All the elves sitting in the council room nodded.

'Why that name?' asked Father Topo, toying with a biscuit.

'My mum and dad used to call me it. When I was a little boy. Because I was born on Christmas Day. It was a nickname.'

'Father Christmas?' said Father Vodol, suspiciously. 'It doesn't sound very memorable.'

'I like it,' said Father Topo. He munched on

his biscuit, getting crumbs in his moustache. 'I mean, you brought Little Kip back on Christmas Day, didn't you? It fits. Father Christmas.'

'Christmas is a time of giving,' said Mother Ri-Ri. 'And you yourself were a gift. A human gift.'

Nikolas felt memories come flooding back. A tear rolled down his cheek.

Father Christmas.

He remembered those early Christmases when his parents had both been alive, and they had gone to sing carols in the town square at Kristiinankaupunki. He remembered the joy of that later Christmas, when his father had shown him the sleigh he had been building and hiding in the forest. Even the turnip-doll had been special at the time.

He smiled, wiping away that happy tear, and sounded the name over in his mind. 'I think Father Christmas is perfect!'

'Hooray,' said Father Topo, swallowing the last of his biscuit. 'This calls for gingerbread!'

A Last Visit to Aunt Carlotta

The first thing Father Christmas did was to undo all the things Father Vodol had done.

'Elves should be free to wear whatever tunic they like,' he said. 'No green tunics and blue tunics and all that. Oh, and they can sit at whichever table they choose. And spickle dancing should be encouraged. And singing can be joyful again, and food be enjoyed . . .'

And the elves of the Elf Council all agreed.

'And there should be joy and goodwill . . .'

'Joy and goodwill!' said Mother Ri-Ri. 'Really? That is a bit controversial.'

'Yes. Maybe it is. But elves used to be happy, and they can be happy again.'

And then came a cry of 'Joy and goodwill!' And everyone was saying it. Well, not everyone. Not solemn-faced Father Vodol for instance. But even he managed to offer a small smile.

Yes, there was no mistaking it. The human

boy had brought happiness back to Elfhelm. And happiness was here to stay.

That evening, Nikolas climbed onto Blitzen's back and went on one last voyage. He wanted to see the house he had left behind. So they flew in a straight line, fast and quick, back to the cottage where he had grown up. They landed next to the well which his mother had fallen into, and he sat on a tree stump that had been chopped by his father. He walked back to the cottage, which still smelt faintly of rotten turnip, and saw Aunt Carlotta wasn't there. He sat inside, and breathed it all in, knowing it would probably be the last time he would come here.

Later, flying back, they saw Aunt Carlotta walking to Kristiinankaupunki. As they flew over her head, she looked up, and Nikolas thought that it would help her a great deal in her life if she could believe in magic. So he shouted at her from a great height.

'Aunt Carlotta! It's me! Flying on a reindeer! I'm all right but I won't be coming home again!'

And Aunt Carlotta looked up, just in time to see Nikolas waving at her in the sky on the back of a reindeer. And to see something brown, streaking fast towards her.

You see, while Nikolas wanted Aunt Carlotta to believe in magic, Blitzen – well, Blitzen had another idea. And he was bang on target too. The reindeer dung landed squarely on her head, and covered her best town clothes.

'You rotten beasts!' she screamed at the sky, clawing the stinking dark stuff off her face.

But by then, Blitzen and Nikolas had disappeared back into the clouds.

How Father Christmas
Spent the Next Ten Years

1. *Eating gingerbread*
Having spent his first eleven years knowing only mushroom soup he spent the next ten years eating the kind of food elves eat. Not only gingerbread but cloudberry jam, blueberry buns, bilberry pie, sweet plum soup, chocolate, jelly, sweets. All the major elf food groups. There was always food to eat, at any time of day.

2. *Growing*
He had grown very tall, double the height of the tallest of all elves, Father Vodol.

3. *Talking to reindeer*
He began to realise that reindeer have their own language. It wasn't a language using their mouths, but it was a language. And he liked nothing more than to go out and talk to them. They talked about the weather a *lot*, had seventeen thousand, five hundred and sixty-three words for moss (but only one for grass), believed antlers explained the universe, loved

flying, and thought humans were just elves that had gone wrong. Prancer was the most talkative, and always told jokes, Donner was always full of compliments, Cupid spoke of love, Vixen was incredibly gloomy and liked asking deep questions ('If a tree falls in a forest, and no one sees it, does it really fall?'), Comet made no sense whatsoever, and Blitzen was always pretty quiet, but Nikolas liked his company best of all.

4. *Working on his image*
Obviously Nikolas needed special clothes, as there wasn't an elf outfit in existence that he could fit into. So Mother Breer made his belts (black leather with a fancy silver buckle) and an elf called Shoehorn (yes, really!) made his boots and the village tailor Father Loopin made his clothes, which were the brightest red.

5. *Wearing a hat*
His father's hat, to be precise. Clean and fresh and alive with colour again.

6. *Being jolly*
Every day, not only did he wear his red and white outfit, complete with shiny black belt

and boots, but he was determined to be as jolly as could be, because the easiest way to make other people happy was to be happy yourself, or at least to act as if you were. That was how his mother had done it. And even his father too, once upon a time.

7. *Writing*
He wrote the three bestselling books of the decade in Elfhelm, selling over twenty-seven copies each. *How to Be Jolly: The Father Christmas Guide to Happiness*, *Sleighcraft for Dummies* and *The Reindeer Whisperer.*

8. *Working*
He worked hard as leader of the Elf Council. He opened nurseries and play parks. Attended every boring meeting. He brokered a peace deal with the trolls. And turned Elfhelm into a happy place of toys and speckle-dancing once more.

9. *Remembering*
He often thought of his father. He also thought of the human world he had left behind, and felt sad that his fellow humans couldn't share the wonders of Elfhelm. He began to think,

gradually, over the years, about whether to take some of the goodness here – some of the magic – and spread it around the human world.

10. *Making friends*
Nikolas had never had friends before. Now he had seven thousand, nine hundred and eighty-three friends. They were mainly elves, but that was okay, because elves were the best kind of friends to have.

Naughty and Nice

Yes. Nikolas made lots of fantastic friends among the elves, and was something of a role model for Little Kip and Little Noosh (who now weren't so little, and were called just Kip and Noosh).

'Why do you think some humans are naughty?' Kip asked him, one day, while Nikolas took him and Noosh out for a sleighcraft lesson. They were all together on the sleigh, which now had a comfy seat made by Father Topo. Kip was handsome, for an elf, with raven-black hair and a dimple in his chin, while Noosh still had a happy wildness to her. She always reminded Nikolas of a warm fire made into an elf.

They were somewhere over Norway. Even though it was the middle of the day it was always safe to fly over Norway, as there were still only eight people living there.

Noosh was holding the reins, staring ahead,

as Blitzen and Donner and all the other reindeer powered through the air.

'Most humans are just a mixture of good things and some bad things,' said Nikolas.

'Like reindeer,' said Noosh.

'I suppose so.'

'But with reindeer it's easy,' said Kip, pulling out a sheet of crumpled paper from his pocket. He handed it to Nikolas. Kip had drawn a line down the middle and on one side put 'Naughty' and on the other 'Nice'.

'Poor Vixen,' said Nikolas, seeing she was the only reindeer in the naughty list.

'Well, she bit Prancer the other day.'

'Did she?'

'But Prancer was on the list last week. Then I told him I'd give him a biscuit if he was good.'

Nikolas thought about this for a little while, but the thought soon melted away, like snow in the sun.

Noosh angled the sleigh, carefully, to avoid an approaching rain cloud. She was the best sleigh rider in Elfhelm now, no doubt about it.

'Why don't you give them some magic? The humans, I mean,' said Noosh.

'Ho ho, Noosh! It's not as easy as that. Come

on, we'd better get back to Elfhelm. Your grandfather will be waiting for you, your parents too, Kip. And these reindeer will be getting hungry.'

'I'm twenty-two next week,' Nikolas told Father Topo, a few minutes after they had landed. They were feeding the reindeer while Noosh and Kip practised their spickle dance moves. Father Topo looked at Nikolas. He had quite a way to look now too, because Nikolas was now over six feet tall. He was taller than his father had been. Yes, Nikolas was a tall, strong, smiling, handsome human, who – despite the smile – always wore a slight frown. As though he was permanently confused about something, a mystery he hadn't quite solved.

'Yes. I know,' said Father Topo, as a breeze tickled his white whiskers.

'Do you think that will be the age I find out who I'm meant to be?'

'Maybe. But you'll know when you find yourself, because then you will stop ageing.'

Nikolas knew this. He knew that anyone with elf magic inside them never grew older than the age where they were truly happy with themselves.

'It took you ninety-nine years, didn't it?'

Father Topo sighed. 'Yes, but that's quite unusual.' He gave Vixen a biscuit. 'There you go, you grumpy thing.'

'But . . .'

'Don't think about it. Look at Blitzen. Look at his antlers. They haven't changed in two years. He has found his perfect age without even thinking about it.'

Nikolas looked back towards the Main Path that led towards

the Street of Seven Curves. He looked at the giant clog hanging outside the clogmakers, and the little spinning top painted onto the sign outside the toymakers. He saw Minmin at her newspaper stall selling the *Daily Snow*. Every elf had

a purpose. Then he turned back to the field, the reindeer and the oval lake – less like a mirror today as the water rippled in the breeze.

'I need to do something. Something big. Something good. There's no point being leader of the elves unless I lead them *somewhere*.'

'Well,' said Father Topo, softly, 'whatever you decide to do, you know all of us will be behind you. Everyone loves you. Everyone is the happiest they have been since Mother Ivy's rule a long time ago. Even Father Vodol quite likes you these days . . .'

Nikolas laughed out loud. 'I can't quite believe that.'

'Oh yes,' said Father Topo. 'The goodness has won in him. And the goodness is spreading far and wide, beyond the village. Have you heard that the pixies don't grow hewlip any more? And there have been no burglaries since Mother Breer had her belts stolen . . . The tower has been empty for a year now and the trolls don't bother us any more, though I think that's because they know you live here, and the story got out. Father Christmas – Troll Killer, ha ha!'

Nikolas nodded and guiltily remembered that day in the tower.

'You'll find something. And it will be

something good. They look up to you. We all do. And not just because you're twice as tall as us!'

Nikolas and Blitzen found this very funny.

'Ho ho ho!' he said, as he gave the reindeer a carrot. Then he thought of something. 'Hmmm, where can I get a telescope?'

How to Be Jolly Even When Times are Bad.

1. Eat more gingerbread, chocolate, jam and cake.

2. Say the word 'Christmas'.

3. Give someone a present. Like a toy, or a book, or a kind word, or a big hug.

4. Laugh, even if there is nothing to laugh about. Especially then.

5. Think of a happy memory. Or a happy future.

6. Wear something red.

7. Believe

(Extract from How to Be Jolly: The Father Christmas Guide to Happiness)

Father Christmas Seeks the Truth

The next day, Nikolas headed into the Wooded Hills with a present. Whenever he saw anyone he hadn't seen for a while he took a present. There was nothing that made him feel better than the simple act of giving. And today the present he was holding was a telescope that had been made by Picklewick, the elf who had once shouted at him when he was up on the roof. He still felt bad about that, no matter how many times Nikolas told him not to.

Anyway, Father Topo had been right. There were no hewlip plants growing on the hills any more. There were still some rough patches of earth that hadn't been replanted, but elsewhere there were just cloudberries and plum trees.

He walked until he reached a yellow cottage with a thatched roof. It was very, very small. He knocked on the door, and waited. Soon a little long-haired, angel-faced pixie appeared.

'Hello, Truth Pixie,' he said.

The creature smiled a wide pixie smile.

'Hello, Nikolas,' she said. 'Or should I call you Father Christmas? Or should I say . . . *Santa Claus*?'

'Santa Claus?' said Nikolas. 'What does that mean?'

The pixie giggled. 'Oh, it's just a name the pixies have for you. The literal translation is "Strange Man with a Big Belly".'

'Charming!' He held out the telescope. 'This is for you. I thought you might like it, especially as you have such good views around here.'

Nikolas felt a tingle of joy as he watched the Truth Pixie's eyes light up.

'A magic viewing stick! How did you know I wanted one?'

'Oh, just a guess.'

The pixie put her eye to the telescope and looked over at Elfhelm. 'Wow! Wow! Everything is the same but bigger!' And then she turned it around and made everything look smaller. 'Ha! Look at you! Little Father Christmas the pixie!'

'Ho ho ho!'

'Anyway, come in! Come in.'

Nikolas squeezed inside the tiny home, into

a yellow room full of pretty pixie plates hanging on the walls. He sat on a little wooden stool, and had to keep his head bent low. The room was warm, and smelt nice. Sugar and cinnamon with maybe a faint tang of cheese.

The pixie smiled.

'What are you smiling about?'

'I think I'm still a bit in love with you. After you saved my life that time.' Her face was reddening. She didn't want to say this, but when you're a Truth Pixie you can't help it. 'I mean, I know it couldn't work out between us. A pixie and a human. You're far too tall and your strange rounded ears would give me nightmares.' She sighed, stared down at the yellow tiled floor. 'I really wish I hadn't said that.'

'That's okay. I'm sure there are plenty of nice pixies out there.'

'No. No. Pixies are surprisingly dull. But the truth is, I like being on my own.'

Nikolas nodded. 'Me too.'

There was a bit of an awkward silence. Not quite a silence, as there was a little scrabbling, munching sound – a sound Nikolas recognised but couldn't work out from where.

'I read about you in the *Daily Snow* all the time. You seem to be quite the celebrity.'

239

'Um, yes.' Nikolas looked through the tiny window, at one of the nicest views of Elfhelm, with the giant mountain in the distance. He looked over at the disused tower. Then he saw a frail old mouse, nibbling on a stinky chunk of troll cheese. That was the sound he had heard.

It couldn't be. But yes, it was. It was Miika.

'Miika. Miika! Is that really you?'

Miika turned his head and looked at Nikolas for a moment.

'Miika, it's you. How wonderful.'

'Actually, his name is Glump,' said the Truth Pixie. 'I found him waiting in my house, after I was released from the tower. He always likes the food I give him. Especially the troll cheese.'

'It's a bit better than turnip, eh?' Nikolas asked the mouse, softly.

'Cheese,' said Miika. 'Cheese is real. I have cheese.'

As Nikolas looked at the mouse he thought back to his childhood over ten years and a whole country away. He thought of his father and his mother and Aunt Carlotta. It was strange. Seeing someone – even a mouse – who had shared the same room as him opened the door to a hundred memories. But Miika didn't seem emotional and kept nibbling his cheese.

'I don't understand,' said the Truth Pixie.

Nikolas was about to tell her that Miika was actually an old friend, but watching the rodent munching happily on the cheese he decided to keep this information to himself. Miika was clearly contented in his woodland home. 'It doesn't matter . . . I hear you pixies aren't being violent any more.'

'Oh,' said the Truth Pixie. 'We still love the *idea* of exploding heads. But you know what? After it happens you feel very empty inside. And anyway, I've invented this . . .'

She went over to a drawer and pulled something out. It was a bright red kind of tube made out of thick paper.

'Hold that end and pull,' she said, holding the other end.

They pulled and there was a mighty BANG!

Miika dropped the cheese then picked it up again in his tiny claws.

The Truth Pixie squealed with delight. 'Don't you just love it?'

'Wow. I wasn't expecting that.'

'I'm calling them "crackers". You can put little presents inside. And less to clear up than with an exploding troll head. Anyway, why are you here?'

'I came to see you because I need to talk to someone who can be honest with me. I can talk to elves, but they're so busy being kind that they're not always so good at being truthful. But you are.'

The tiny creature nodded. 'Truth is what I do.'

Nikolas hesitated. He felt slightly embarrassed. He was so big and tall, compared to a mouse and a pixie, yet the mouse and the pixie knew exactly who and what they were. They had found their place in the world. 'The thing is . . . I am human, sort of, but I have magical abilities too. I am Nikolas. But I am now also Father Christmas. I am very in-between. But it's difficult. I am told that I just need to work out what I want to do. The elves say I do good. But what good do I do?'

'You set up Goodwill day, in honour of Mother Ivy. You've allowed spickle dancing. You've given all the elves more chocolate money. You opened the new elf nursery. And the play park. And the clog museum. And turned the prison back into the Welcome Tower. Your books are still doing well. Not that I really like that elf-help nonsense. You passed your sleighcraft exam. You teach young elves how to fly sleighs.'

'*Everyone* passes their sleighcraft exam. And yes, I do a bit of teaching, but I don't know if that's my destiny.'

The Truth Pixie tried to think. 'You saved Little Kip.'

'Ten years ago.'

'Yes, perhaps you are living on past glories, just a little bit,' said the Truth Pixie, solemnly. 'But the elves do admire you.'

'I know they respect me. But they shouldn't. They need a purpose. A true purpose. I haven't given them that.'

The Truth Pixie thought about this, and waited for the truth to come. This took a moment or two. Three moments, in fact. Then she had it.

'Sometimes,' she said, as her eyes shone wide and bright, 'people look up to people not for who they have been, but for what they could become. For what they know they could be. They see in you something special.'

Miika had finished his cheese now, and scuttled over to the end of the little table. He jumped onto Nikolas's lap.

'Oh, he likes you,' said the Truth Pixie. 'That's

rare. He's normally quite picky. Look, he's looking up to you. Just like the elves do.'

'I do like you,' said Miika, in his quiet mouse language, 'even though you are not a dairy product.'

'Everyone looks up to you.'

As the Truth Pixie spoke, Nikolas felt something stir inside him. That warm, sweet feeling. The feeling of magic and hope and kindness that was the very best feeling in the world. It told him, once again, what he had known now for ten years. *Nothing was impossible.* But even better than that, he now had a sense that he was in Elfhelm for a reason. He might never be able to be a true elf. But he was here now, and like everything in life there was a purpose at work.

'You have the power to do good, and you know it.'

He *did* know he had the power to do good, and he would find a way to do it. A way to unite the Nikolas side of himself and the Father Christmas side. He would unite the human bits with the magical bits, and maybe one day he could change not just Elfhelm but the lives of humans too.

The Truth Pixie screwed up her nose. Her

triangular little face was lost in thought. Then from out of nowhere she shouted a word into the air. 'Giving!'

'What?'

'Giving is what makes you happy. I saw your face when you gave me the viewing stick. It was still a big strange human face but it was so happy!'

Nikolas smiled and rubbed his chin. 'Giving, yes. Giving . . . Thank you, Truth Pixie. I owe you the whole world.'

The Truth Pixie smiled some more. 'This humble cottage and these Wooded Hills are enough for me.'

Then Miika crawled across Nikolas's knee and wanted to jump on the floor, so Nikolas held out his hand for the mouse to climb on, and gently lowered him to the ground. 'Cheese is better than turnip, isn't it?' said Nikolas.

'It most certainly is,' said Miika. And Nikolas seemed to understand.

Nikolas got off the tiny chair and crouched his way out of the tiny house.

The Truth Pixie thought of something as Nikolas made his way down the hill towards Elfhelm. 'Oh, and you should grow a beard! It would really suit you.'

Forty years later . . .

FATHER CHRISTMAS REVEALS ALL IN

PRICE 2 CHOCOLATE COINS

The Daily Snow

EVERY ELF'S FAVOURITE NEWSPAPER

EXCLUSIVE: FATHER CHRISTMAS REVEALS HIS NEW LOOK

Father Christmas was spotted at Reindeer Field this weekend with a beard.

Speaking to the Daily Snow's political correspondent, Mother Jingle, Father Christmas commented 'Yes, it's true. This is a beard and it's on my face. But I really want to talk about the need for more goodwill and ...

So there you have it. Father Christmas's beard is real.

See pages 33 to 47 for advice on
HOW TO GET THE FATHER CHRISTMAS LOOK

The Magic of Giving

It takes some people a long time to work out exactly what they are here for. In Nikolas's case it took him another forty years.

He was now sixty-two years old. He had not only kept his beard, as the Truth Pixie suggested, but he had been leader of the Elf Council for A Very Long Time.

In that time he had preserved and expanded happiness in Elfhelm. He had started a weekly spickle dance (with singing Tomtegubbs) in the village hall, given free toys to every newborn elf, converted the tower into a toy workshop, established a University of Advanced Toymaking, expanded the School of Sleighcraft, set up the Pixie–Elf alliance, signed a peace treaty with the trolls, invented the mince pie, and sherry, and gingerbread men, and had raised the elf minimum wage to five hundred chocolate coins a week.

But he still felt he needed to do more. He knew he needed to do more because he was

still getting older by the day. Most elves –
with the exception of Father Topo and a few
others – had stopped ageing at around forty,
and it was getting a bit silly. He was taking
so long to find his purpose. He loved helping
the elves, but it was time to help the people
that part of him still belonged to. The people
he had left behind in their world, one that
was too often full of loss and pain and sadness.
He could sense them. He would lie awake
in bed at night and hear their voices in his
head. He could feel the whole world in there.
The good and the bad. The naughty and the
nice.

One Sunday night in spring, when there was
no moon, he took Blitzen from the field and
flew beyond the mountain.

There was no better feeling than flying
through the sky on the back of a reindeer.
Even after a lifetime of doing so, Nikolas –
who was now so comfortable with the name
Father Christmas he called himself Father
Christmas – loved the magical feeling of
zooming through the sky. They kept flying.
Right across Finland, across the forest where
he last saw his father, searching for him, the
way he always searched for him whenever he

flew. It was foolish. His father had died long ago, but it was an old habit. They flew on into southern Denmark, over towns and cities, over the small fishing port of Helsinki, where trawlers and other boats waited for the fishermen who would take them out onto the rough seas again.

Father Christmas desperately wanted to speak to one of his own kind, but he had long vowed to the elves that he would keep their secret. He knew they were right. Humans probably still couldn't be trusted to know about elves and their magic. But that was only because human lives could be so hard.

On and on they flew, over the kingdom of Hanover, the Netherlands and France. The lands below were all dark, but with brief bursts of light from all the fires and the gas streetlamps that glimmered in the cities below. As Father Christmas finally asked Blitzen to head home, he thought all of human life – and certainly the life he remembered – was like this landscape. Dark, with occasional bursts of light.

As he flew back north, under the moonless sky, he realised that although he might not have been able to live with the humans again, the question still bothered him: how could he make their lives better? Happier?

The following day he asked that very same question in a meeting of the Elf Council.

'We need to find a way to spread as much happiness as possible,' he announced.

Father Vodol arrived a bit late, clutching a stack of presents.

'Happy birthday, Father Vodol!' said Father Christmas.

They all sang 'Happy Birthday'. When Father Vodol was seated he turned and smiled at his good friend, Father Christmas, and wished he could turn back time and change that day he had put him in prison.

'But everyone is happy,' said Mother Noosh, who was now a successful journalist, as the *Daily Snow*'s chief reindeer correspondent.

'Everyone *here* is still happy,' corrected Father Christmas. 'But I want to spread that happiness beyond the mountain.'

There was a collective gasp from everyone who was there, which wasn't many, as there was a cake-eating competition going on downstairs in the village hall.

'Beyond the mountain?' asked Father Topo. 'But it's too dangerous. Everything is perfect here. If we let all the humans know we are here it would be chaos! No offence, Father Christmas.'

Father Christmas nodded thoughtfully and scratched his beard, which was now as white as Father Topo's whiskers. Father Topo always had a point and this was no exception.

'I agree, Father Topo, I agree. But what if we did something that gave just a little bit of magic? Something that could brighten their lives?'

'But what?' asked Father Vodol, who was opening a birthday present. 'A cuddly toy reindeer!' he squealed with joy. 'It looks just like Blitzen! Thank you, Father Christmas.'

'A pleasure,' said Father Christmas.

And Father Christmas watched that joy on Father Vodol's face, and thought – as he often did – about the magic of giving. He thought of the day he had been given the sledge. And the time, a few years later, when he had been given the turnip-doll. Even though a sleigh is significantly better than a turnip, the feeling of receiving both had been the same. The Truth Pixie had been right. Giving was what he was good at.

And then that night, at around midnight, it came to him.

It was the biggest and craziest idea he had ever had in his life.

The idea would involve a lot of things. First of all, a lot of hard work. But elves loved work – if it was fun – so he would make sure it *was* fun. It had to be fun, because if they weren't having fun then it would go badly wrong. He would convert the tower from merely being a toy workshop to being the greatest toy workshop imaginable.

The plan would also involve reindeer. Yes, all of the reindeer would be needed. He would need Blitzen to lead the way, because no one was as good in the air as Blitzen. He was not only strong and quick, but he also had determination. He would never leave a journey half finished, just as Nikolas would never leave a mountain half climbed. As well as Blitzen, he would need Donner at the front to help with navigation. Or maybe that new reindeer Mother Noosh found wandering the Wooded Hills. The one with the strange red nose.

And they'd need a good sleigh. They'd need the best sleigh there had ever been, in fact. He'd need to recruit the best sleighmakers. He would need it to be strong and streamlined and silent through the air.

But there was still a problem. He paced his bedroom, munching on chocolate. He looked out of his window, past Blitzen and the other eight reindeer asleep in the dark, over to the village hall. He looked at the new clock face. Fifteen minutes had gone by since he'd first had the idea. Time moved so quickly.

He'd need to do something about that.

About time.

How could he travel to every child in the world in a single night? It was impossible.

But Father Topo's words from long ago came back to him.

An impossibility is just a possibility you don't understand.

He looked to the sky and saw a comet's fiery trail as it made its path between the stars, before fading away into the night like a dream.

'A shooting star,' he said to himself, remembering the one he had seen with Miika all those years ago.

'I do believe in magic, Miika,' he said,

imagining the long gone mouse was still there with him. 'Just as you believed in cheese.'

And where there was magic, there was always a way.

And this time he knew he would find it. He stayed up all night thinking about it, and then he stopped thinking about it and started believing in it. He believed it so completely that it was already real. There was no use trying to *think* of a way, because it was impossible. And the only way you could make something impossible real wasn't through logic or sensible thinking. No. It was to *believe* it could be done. Belief was the method. You could stop time, expand chimneys, even travel the world in a single night, with the right magic and belief inside you.

And it was going to happen at Christmas.

And the moment he knew it he felt a warm glow. It started in his tummy and spread through his whole body. It was the feeling that comes when you find out who you really are, and who you know you will be. And in finding himself he had stopped growing old right there. The way you stop when you reach a destination after a long journey, or after reaching the last page in a book, when the story is complete and stays that way for ever. And so he knew that he – the man called Christmas, who really still felt as young as ever, a sixty-two year old *boy* called Christmas – wouldn't age another day.

He picked up his father's old red hat. He placed it to his face and was sure he could smell the scent of pines from the old forest where his father had spent every day chopping down so many trees. He put the hat on his head, then he heard the distant sound of voices coming from the village hall. Of course! It was Monday. Dance night. He opened his window wide and saw hundreds of happy elves walking back to their homes. He felt such a joyous spirit inside himself he leant out of the window and shouted as loud as he could.

'Merry Christmas to all, and to all a good night!'

And everyone looked up at him, and without question said, 'Merry Christmas!'

And everyone – including Father Christmas – laughed.

'Ho ho ho!'

And so it was that he closed the window and finished his chocolate and went to bed.

He closed his eyes and smiled with such joy, thinking of all the magic and wonder he would share next Christmas.

PRICE 2 CHOCOLATE COINS

The Daily Snow

EVERY ELF'S FAVOURITE NEWSPAPER

FATHER CHRISTMAS'S BIG GAMBLE

After months of intense preparation, Father Christmas reported today at the toy workshop that plans were going well.

'Everything is on track', he told the Daily Snow's political correspondent Mother Jingle.

'We had a little crisis earlier in the month with missing jigsaw pieces but that has been resolved.' — CONTINUED ON PAGES 2-3

The First Child to Wake Up

The very first child to wake on Christmas morning was an eight-year-old girl called Amelia who lived in a small house on the outskirts of London in the grey and rainy country known as England.

She opened her eyes and stretched. She heard her mother coughing through the wall. She saw something in the darkness of her room. An unmoving shape at the end of her bed. The sight made her curious. She sat up. And there was a stocking bulging with parcels.

She unwrapped the first parcel, her heart racing.

'Impossible,' she said, opening it up. It was a little wooden horse. Exactly what she had always wanted. She opened the next present. A spinning top, perfectly hand-painted with the most lively pattern of zigzags. Something else. A little orange! She had never seen an orange before. And money made out of chocolate!

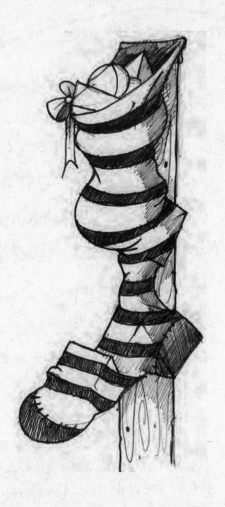

She noticed a piece of cream writing paper folded up in the bottom of the stocking. She began to read:

Dear Amelia,

I am pleased to tell you that you have been a GOOD GIRL this year.

I hope you enjoy the presents. The elves made them especially for you.

My name is Father Christmas.

When I was your age I was called Nikolas.

There will be alot of people in your life who will tell you to 'grow up' or to insist that you stop believing in magic.

Do NOT listen to these people.

There IS magic in this world. And me and the elves and some fine flying reindeer will prove it to you, and all the children of the world, every Christmas morning, when you find a stocking full of presents.

Now, go and spread the word.

Merry Christmas!

Yours F.C.

Acknowledgements

Every book is a team effort and this book is no exception. So here is the *A Boy Called Christmas* 'Nice List'.

I would like to thank –
Chris Mould, for turning my words into fantastic pictures. Francis Bickmore, Head Elf, for helping make the words better. Jamie Byng, the Santa of Canongate. Jenny Todd, Mother Christmas. Rafaela Romaya, Sian Gibson and all the elves in the Canongate workshop. Kirsten Grant and Matthew Railton for getting the snowball rolling. Clare Conville, for sprinkling her pixie dust on my working life. Camilla Young and Nick Marston for their festive film wisdom.Everyone at Conville and Walsh and Curtis Brown. All the film folk at Blueprint Pictures and Studio Canal for their joy and goodwill. All the wonderful booksellers that spend their lives spreading the miracle of books, and not just at Christmas. My soulmate Andrea Semple, for helping in infinite ways on this book, and for turning my world into something magical.

THE NEW MAGICAL STORY FROM

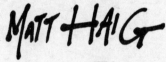

FROM THE BESTSELLING AUTHOR OF
A Boy Called Christmas

A Mouse Called Miika

Matt Haig

with illustrations by Chris Mould

CANON║GATE

A Tale of Two Mice

Two mice were sitting in a forest, leaning against a pine cone.

They were friends. And they looked quite ordinary. They had ordinary dark eyes, ordinary pink noses, ordinary tails.

Where they lived, though, was quite *un*-ordinary. Because where they lived was the Far North.

At the very top of a country that humans call Finland is a little town called Elfhelm, which is the most unique place on the whole planet. A place you won't find on any map. A place full of brightly coloured wooden houses in winding streets. A place full of elves, and flying reindeer, and the occasional pixie.

One of the mice was called Miika. He was the less scruffy of the two, but still a little bit scruffy. His brown fur was often dotted with mushroom crumbs on his chest and tummy. Unlike his friend, Miika liked the elves, the reindeer and the pixies of Elfhelm.

'I'm glad I found you,' he said, gazing through the snow-dusted trees.

'And why is that, Miika?' sighed the mouse with mud on her fur and frost on her whiskers, as if she'd heard the words many times before. The one whose name was Bridget the Brave. Well, really she was just called Bridget, but she always made Miika (and everyone else) call her Bridget the Brave. Because she was that sort of mouse. A mouse with attitude.

'Because I don't feel alone any more. I have found someone who is just like me.'

Bridget the Brave laughed. She looked past the tall pines, down towards the colourful wooden houses of the elf village that she hated so much. 'You're not like me, Miika.'

'Why not?'

'Well,' she said, 'I am Bridget the Brave. I am fearless. You are not. That's one difference.'

Miika wanted to ask in what other ways they were different. But he was too scared. So he just sat there, staring at the mushroom in front of him, and remembered his early life, when he lived in a dark and damp tree hole . . .

THE NEXT BRILLIANT STORIES
IN THE FESTIVE SERIES

MEGA
Matt Haig
FESTIVE

ACTIVITIES

Father Christmas has got all of these Christmassy words jumbled up in the elves' workshop – can you help him to find them again?

C	V	S	L	E	I	G	H	K	V	L	T	Y	S	M	S
F	I	B	G	L	F	C	A	B	W	N	O	N	G	F	P
P	A	Z	R	E	I	B	A	S	O	W	J	N	I	C	I
W	A	T	X	E	L	J	Y	V	Q	A	P	U	N	R	C
O	R	U	H	O	Y	F	U	B	O	H	Y	B	G	S	K
N	G	E	W	E	R	G	H	X	G	M	K	R	E	Z	L
S	Z	X	T	M	R	Y	A	E	P	S	H	E	R	X	E
V	C	O	A	U	H	C	R	U	L	A	Y	T	B	T	D
K	A	F	R	Q	T	J	H	E	L	M	X	S	R	V	A
N	M	X	Q	E	S	T	D	R	D	Q	E	A	E	C	N
F	E	H	I	N	I	F	C	J	I	T	N	E	A	U	C
N	L	D	W	U	R	N	B	V	P	S	E	D	D	L	I
T	I	X	T	O	W	B	D	Z	I	Y	T	A	Q	E	N
Q	A	B	K	C	F	M	R	E	P	H	K	M	W	P	G
D	J	F	S	E	R	D	U	G	E	W	E	D	A	L	Z
M	A	G	I	C	K	M	G	N	J	R	I	M	L	S	H

Elfhelm   Reindeer   Magic
Gingerbread Snow   Easter Bunny
Father Christmas Sleigh
Amelia   Spickledancing

Find out more at kids.matthaig.com

Nikolas has got lost in the forest. Can you help him find his way back home to Elfhelm, without stumbling across any bunnies or down any holes?

FINISH

START

Find out more at kids.matthaig.com

CANON GATE

SPOT THE DIFFERENCE

Can you spot the differences between these characters from
The Truth Pixie? There are five to find on each character . . .

Find out more at kids.matthaig.com

CANON‖GATE